"I'm so ashamed, Mike."

The luscious blonde named Sheila Martin was eager to get everything off her chest. That was why she made a midnight date to meet Mike Shayne alone in his apartment.

In a choking voice she admitted the things Wanda Weatherby had made her do in front of the cameras when Sheila had been a young, innocent girl.

Sheila was still young, still beautiful, but a lot less innocent—guilty, in fact, of almost anything but murder. At least that's what she said. And if Mike wanted convincing, she was very willing to try. . . .

what really happened

BRETT HALLIDAY

A DELL BOOK

For Tempa Thomas

Published by
DELL PUBLISHING CO., INC.
750 Third Avenue
New York, N.Y. 10017
Copyright © 1952 by Brett Halliday
All rights reserved
Dell ® TM 681510, Dell Publishing Co., Inc.
Reprinted by arrangement with
Dodd, Mead & Company
New York, N.Y.
Printed in the U.S.A.
Previous Dell Edition #9458
New Dell Edition
First printing—February 1970

CHAPTER ONE

MICHAEL SHAYNE HEARD his telephone ringing when he stopped in the corridor and put the key in the lock of his apartment door. The time was a little past nine-thirty, and he felt whipped down, ready for a nightcap and bed.

He frowned at the insistent ringing as he walked in and switched on the light. His first impulse was to ignore it, but the boy at the switchboard had seen him come through the lobby, and Shayne knew he would keep ringing until it was answered.

As it was, he took his time. He tossed his hat on a hook near the door, yawned widely, and ran a big-fingered hand through coarse red hair as he crossed to the wall cabinet and took down a bottle of cognac. He filled a three-ounce glass, let half the liquor trickle warmly down his throat, and with bottle and glass in his hands he recrossed the room to his desk. Thumping the bottle down, he lifted the receiver, said, "Shayne speaking," and took another sip of cognac.

The answering voice was a surly growl. "Is that Mike Shayne, the shamus?"

Shayne hesitated, scowling heavily and taking the receiver from his ear as though to return it to its prongs. Then he lifted one shoulder slightly and said, "This is Michael Shayne. Who's speaking?"

"Never mind that. You wouldn't know my name nohow, shamus. I got this here message and you better listen *clost* because it's on the line." There was a pause which Shayne assumed was intended to impress him with the seriousness of the message to follow. Then: "Lay off Wanda Weatherby."

The rangy detective's ragged red brows rose slightly. He said, "Who?"

"Wanda Weatherby. That dame's dynamite—to *you.* Lay off her, see?"

"I can't very well lay off her," said Shayne easily. "I never heard of her. What in hell is all this about?"

"Wanda Weatherby," the surly voice said. "A dame. You'll be gettin' a letter from her, but if you're smart like they say, you'll tear it up without readin' it and stay clear of her."

Shayne said, "Nuts," and hung up. Again he yawned, and looked at his watch. The time was nine forty-two. He finished his cognac, loosened his tie, and began unbuttoning his shirt.

The telephone rang immediately. He let it ring twice before answering. The same voice complained, "We was cut off, I reckon."

Shayne said, "I hung up."

"I thought maybe you did." The man sounded perturbed and slightly regretful. "The boss ain't gonna like it if I tell him you didn't get the whole message. God knows why he wants to give a lousy shamus like you a chance to keep on livin', but he does. He's funny that way. He says to tell you it'd worry his conscience if you got bumped off without askin' for it. But if you ask for it you'll get it, see?"

Shayne growled, "Tell your boss—"

"I'm tellin' *you.*" The receiver clicked at the other end of the wire.

Shayne slowly replaced the receiver and absently tugged

at the lobe of his left ear. Wanda Weatherby? The name was one that would stick in a man's memory. He was quite sure he had never heard it before. He shrugged his wide shoulders in a gesture of dismissal. What the hell? Miami was full of dames he didn't know. Hundreds of thousands who came every year looking for thrills. A certain per cent was bound to get into trouble.

He strode into the kitchenette and took out a tray of ice cubes, ran warm water over them, dislodged half a dozen, and put them into a tall glass. He filled the glass with water and returned to his desk where he refilled a smaller glass with cognac. Settling himself in the ancient, creaky swivel chair, he leaned back and crossed his long legs comfortably. He lit a cigarette and blew out a long puff of smoke. Pleasantly relaxed now, he had forgotten about getting to bed early.

The telephone rang for the third time. Shayne grinned. This would be the boss, he told himself, with some more mysterious hocus-pocus about Wanda Weatherby—a woman he didn't know. He hunched forward and picked up the receiver, then swiveled back to say curtly, "Mike Shayne speaking."

"Hello. Is this Michael Shayne? The private detective?"

Shayne's left brow went up. This was a woman's voice. Sensuous and sultry and flowing over the wire. A brunettish sort of voice, he thought. He said, "Yes."

"I'm Mrs. Martin." There was a suggestion of a question mark in her tone.

Again he said, "Yes?" interrogatively.

"*Sheila* Martin, Mr. Shayne."

Shayne swore under his breath. She sounded as though she expected him to remember her. During the pause he rubbed his lean jaw with his free hand and realized that he had never met a woman named Sheila in the flesh. Only in books where they were green-eyed and lovely and improbably sexy. While he was wondering what color her eyes were, she continued.

"I guess you haven't heard from Wanda?"

"No," Shayne admitted. "I haven't heard from Wanda."

The catch in her voice came over the wire, and she said urgently, rapidly, "I have to see you, Mr. Shayne. Please. Tonight. It's terribly important."

He said, "I've just settled down with a drink."

"Of your favorite cognac?"

Shayne sensed the effort to make her voice light, for he knew she was worried, and frightened. He glanced at his glass and said, "Croizet," and took an approving sip.

"I've been trying to reach you for the past hour," Sheila Martin said, her voice urgent again. "I can't—get away right now—but would midnight be too late?"

"For what?"

"I can't explain over the telephone, Mr. Shayne. It's—well—risky. I might be overheard. I can't get away right now. Would you mind dreadfully if I came there about twelve?"

"I wouldn't mind at all, Sheila."

"You're wonderful," she breathed. "I— You *will* be alone, won't you?"

"Definitely."

"I'll see you then, Michael Shayne."

From another woman the last words would have been a coo. From Sheila Martin they were provocative, promising.

She wasn't young, he thought, as he hung up and swayed back in the swivel chair. Old enough to dispense with coyness. Young enough to use her sex appeal to get what she wanted from a man. He alternately sipped cognac and ice water, and idly hoped that she wanted something important from him. But in spite of his mood, he wondered whether she was the boss who wanted him to have no part of Wanda Weatherby.

Shayne slid down in the chair, rested his head on the hard back, and put his big feet up on the table, a glass in each hand. He closed his eyes between sips, and the telephone calls did slow somersaults in his relaxed mind. He was wondering who the devil Wanda Weatherby was when the telephone rang for the fourth time.

He jerked forward, swung his feet to the floor, and picked up the receiver fast. Before he finished saying, "Shayne speaking," a woman's voice broke in, high-pitched, hysterical. Her words rushed into his ear explosively, as though they had been long pent up.

"Mr. Shayne, this is Wanda Weatherby and you don't know my name but I tried to call you twice today and then wrote you a letter you'll get in the morning. I thought I could wait until then but now I'm just frightened to death and I'll die if you don't help me."

Into the silence while she caught her breath, Shayne asked, "What are you afraid—"

"Please don't interrupt me," she screamed. "It's a life-or-death matter, and I'll be holding my breath until you get here. Please hurry! West Seventy-Fifth Street." She gave him a street number not far from Miami Avenue and hung up before he could ask another question.

Shayne sat erect and very still after he cradled the receiver, a deep frown between his ragged red brows. He looked at his watch. The time was two minutes after ten.

Inured by frantic calls for many years from people of both sexes and all ages, Shayne was inclined to say to hell with Wanda Weatherby and settle back comfortably to await his midnight appointment with Sheila Martin. Apparently she knew what all the excitement was about and could explain it. When he had a few facts to go on—

He leaned back in his chair again and tried to relax, but the memory of the terror in the voice of his last caller brought him up sharply. She had put him on the spot by hanging up before he could refuse. Now he was committed, unless he could call her back and say that he had no intention of dashing out to Seventy-Fifth Street without some sort of explanation.

Leafing through the telephone book to the W's, he realized that he had also been put on the spot by the first telephone call warning him to stay away from Wanda Weatherby. There weren't many Weatherbys listed, and none at the address she had given him. He called Information, and finished his drink while she checked and reported no listing for a Weatherby at that address.

Shayne rebuttoned his shirt and adjusted his tie, and had his hat on and his hand on the doorknob when the telephone rang again. He whirled angrily, strode back to grab the receiver and bark his name into it.

Timothy Rourke, the *Daily News* reporter, answered. "Mike, this is Tim. Are you doing anything?"

"Just spending a quiet evening with my telephone," he said ironically.

"Look, Mike, have you ever heard of a gal named Wanda Weatherby?"

"I haven't heard anything else all evening. What sort of game is this?"

"Is it a game?" The reporter sounded confused. "How about coming over here if you're not busy? Or, we can come over to your place. A friend of mine is in pretty much of a mess, Mike."

"With Wanda?" Shayne asked grimly.

"Yeh. That is— Well, I think you'd better hear it from him, Mike. Shall we come over?"

"I'm on my way out. Where are you, Tim?"

"Here at Ralph's place. Ralph Flannagan. Apartment twenty-six in the Courtland Arms."

That was in the Forties, Shayne figured hastily, on his way back from the address Wanda had given him. He said, "Stay there, Tim, and I'll drop in presently." He hung up and got out of the apartment fast, before the telephone could ring again—with maybe J. Edgar Hoover calling to say that Wanda Weatherby was actually Mrs. Joseph Stalin in disguise. He slammed the door hard behind him as he went out.

In the hotel-apartment lobby he waved to the boy at the switchboard and said, "Take any messages until I get back, Dick. By midnight, I hope," and strode on to the garage at the rear of the building.

As he drove northward toward Seventy-Fifth Street, the name of Ralph Flannagan bothered him. One of Tim Rourke's friends, but that didn't mean much. As a reporter on one of Miami's leading newspapers, it was Tim's business to make friends—particularly when his thin, twitching nose smelled a story in the air.

Shayne knew a moment of indecision, but once more the memory of Wanda's tragic appeal kept him on a direct route, instead of veering off to Flannagan's place. Traffic was light as he drove farther north, and he increased his speed. The moon was a little more than half full above fleecy clouds, and its faint light outlined the quiet residential section of the city as he turned west on Seventy-Fifth and crossed Miami Avenue.

The palm-lined subdivision was sparsely built, the

streets empty of traffic, and the bungalows were dark and silent. Shayne drove slowly, counting the blocks as he passed. When he reached the one he sought, light shone from one house on the right. He pulled up to the curb, stopped in front of it, and sat for a moment looking around.

The one-story, stuccoed bungalow stood well back from the street with some fifty feet of smooth lawn on both sides leading away to tall hibiscus hedges separating the grounds from neighbors, and giving an unusual degree of privacy for so small a dwelling in Miami. The other two homes were in darkness, as were the two across the street.

The house number was easily discernible in phosphorous paint above a low stake at the edge of the lawn, confirming Shayne's guess that this was the right address. He got out of the car and went up the concrete walk to the front door where a dim light outlined the electric button. He pressed it and heard the ringing inside.

He waited, taking out a cigarette and lighting it. There was no sound from within. As he smoked, the utter silence of the neighborhood grew oppressive, and Shayne caught himself straining to hear the sound of Wanda Weatherby's footsteps inside.

He pressed the bell again, holding his finger on it for a long time. When he removed it and the ringing stopped, the night silence seemed more oppressive. He waited a long moment, taking a deep drag on his cigarette, then stepped back to look searchingly at the two big picture windows on either side of the door.

Thick, creamy drapes were carefully drawn across both, and it was impossible to see inside. He spun his cigarette to the lawn and followed a narrow concrete walk around to the side of the house.

The first window he reached was wide open to catch the night breeze, the shade rolled up and the drapes thrust aside. Only a copper screen was between him and a glimpse into the room.

Bright light from a floor lamp at the end of the couch outlined the body of a woman lying face down on the rug, some ten feet beyond the window. A mass of reddish-gold hair obliterated her features from the window view.

Something else reddish was visible in the light. A pool of it spread out around her head, and Shayne knew now why Wanda Weatherby had not answered the doorbell.

Instinctively, he looked at his watch. The time was exactly 10:38.

CHAPTER TWO

SHAYNE'S GRAY EYES were bleak, and a muscle twitched in his lean jaw. He stepped away from the lighted window and lit a cigarette. A feeling of revulsion came over him, followed by an outraged sense of disapproval and disappointment. He had been exceedingly curious about Wanda Weatherby—who she was and what she wanted from him, and what she meant to the other persons who had contacted him earlier.

Now she wouldn't be able to tell him. She couldn't answer any of the questions that had boiled up in his thoughts as he drove toward the address she had given him. It was now abundantly clear that she had good reason for the hysterical panic in her voice when she pleaded with him to come to her.

Thirty minutes had made the difference. She had said that it was a matter of life or death, he recalled grimly. But she could not have realized how close she was shading it, or she would certainly have made the appeal even more urgent. Yet, she had been just about as urgent as a woman could possibly be. She had hung up before he could argue with her, leaving it strictly up to him to get there in time to save her from the death she had reason to fear.

Standing there on the lush green lawn, he was conscious of the quiet, serene beauty of the moonlit night and the cool, humid breeze on his face. It seemed incongruous that a woman lay dead inside the house. His mouth tightened, and he berated himself for not being fast enough. He had wasted five, maybe ten minutes trying to check her phone number to call her back. And then there had been Rourke's call. Another two or three minutes' delay. At a time when minutes were precious!

He whirled suddenly as a thought struck him, dropping his cigarette to the grass. He knew, from long observation and experience that Wanda Weatherby was dead, but the urge to get in to her seized him, to see if there was anything that could possibly be done for her.

Going back to the screen, he reached out a big hand to rip it out. He stopped when he saw the small round hole in almost the exact center of the wire just above the frame. It was not necessarily fresh, and it wasn't necessarily a bullet hole, but that's what it looked like. He withdrew his hand before touching the frame, turned, and went swiftly around to the rear of the bungalow.

Two wide concrete steps led up to the kitchen door. The screen was unlatched, opening outward, but the wooden door with glassed upper portion didn't open when he turned the knob. He hit the thin glass with his elbow, stepped back to let it clatter to the floor, then reached in and turned the key.

The door opened into a dark kitchen. Shayne prowled across the linoleum toward a dim rectangle of light marking the entrance to the dining-room, and found the wall switch. He flipped it and strode on through a pantry lined on both sides with glass doors, behind which crystal and hand-painted dishes and silver gleamed.

He didn't pause or slacken his long-legged strides, but he noted the expensive furnishings in the dining-room. The thick rug, the shining mahogany table centering it, the crystal bowl filled with fresh roses, the four silver candlesticks arranged in perfect symmetry—all outlined by light from the open archway leading into the living-room.

After assuring himself that Wanda Weatherby had been dead for at least half an hour, he straightened up and looked around. There was a fireplace to the left of the window through which he had peered, cozily equipped with antique andirons, a hearth brush, and an attractive basket filled with wood. Two wing chairs stood, one on either side, each with its small, inlaid table holding an ash tray and silver cigarette box. A long period couch with a low back, elaborately carved above the tapestried cushions, ranged along the space beneath the big picture window.

Wanda Weatherby lay on an expensive Herat rug that reached from the hearth to the opposite wall, and directly in front of the couch near the end table which held the telephone. She wore a sea-green hostess gown with a tight bodice brocaded with dull-gold threads, and the full skirt spread out around her slim body as though she had pivoted suddenly, billowing it out, then dropped to the rug, and the fullness had settled just above her bare ankles. The left foot was crossed over the right and was bare. The toes were curled downward in an attitude of agony which had allowed the dull-gold mule to drop from her foot.

Otherwise, her appearance was composed. Her right arm was outstretched above her head with slender, tapering fingers lying flat and relaxed. The left hand was curved beneath her breast.

Studying the body intently, standing less than two feet away, Shayne could now see a large, bloody hole high in the back of her head which was not quite hidden by the thick reddish-gold ringlets.

A soft-nosed bullet, he surmised, entering from the front and ranging upward to emerge at that spot.

He moved to stand directly in line with the prone body and the screened window, gauging the position of the hole in the wire, then pivoting slowly in an arc of one hundred and eighty degrees. From this position he carefully examined the rug, and nodded with satisfaction when he saw the small, shapeless mass of a mushroomed bullet lying three feet away.

Shayne studied the bullet moodily, but it didn't tell him anything except that Wanda Weatherby had been shot through the screen, probably from a rifle, just as she arose from the couch after telephoning him. She had heard a sound and turned toward the window, and then—

He shook his red head slowly. That must have been the way it happened. The pool of blood had glazed over, confirming his first guess as to the time of her murder. Just about the length of time that had elapsed since her telephone call and the time of his arrival.

He tried to visualize the whole scene—the telephone call, her extreme panic. There was something about it that worried him. She hadn't made it sound so imminent, or was he growing callous to frantic women calling him at all times of the night? She had been frightened, but not by something she expected to happen before he could reach her. He was certain of that as he searched his memory for the exact words she had spoken, and the intonations.

No. She had hung up on him, and, somehow, this fact gave Shayne a certain sense of release from his feeling of guilty negligence. If she had heard any suspicious noise outside before or during her brief conversation, she would have told him or screamed, or perhaps fainted from fear and left the receiver dangling.

But she had hung up.

Another twinge of conscience struck him when he remembered that she had tried to reach him by telephone twice that day, and he had not been on the job. The motive for her letter which would reach him in the morning mail was clear. The letter which he had been warned to tear up without reading it if he wanted to stay alive. The letter that a woman named Sheila Martin wanted to talk to him about at midnight, and which a friend of Timothy Rourke's was now waiting to discuss with him.

Only they had the answers now. Wanda Weatherby had made her final pitch half an hour ago when she telephoned him with her urgent plea for help.

Shayne shook his head angrily and ran troubled fingers through his coarse red hair. He went to the telephone. As he lifted the receiver he noticed that there was no number in the blank inside the dial.

That meant the telephone was unlisted and explained why he had been unable to obtain her number from the directory or from Information. This seemed odd for a woman who lived in a small bungalow on a quiet side street.

He dialed police headquarters. At this point, the homicide squad could accomplish a lot more than he could.

CHAPTER THREE

UTILIZING THE BRIEF INTERVAL before the nearest radio police car could reach the scene, Shayne hurried from the death room, went down the narrow hallway to the rear bedroom. It was a small room, with a single bed, unmade, with rumpled sheet and spread thrown back. The drapes at the two windows were drawn aside and hung limply. A cheap, soiled rug lay beside the bed, and when Shayne examined the closet, he found it empty. The only other article of furniture in the room was a substantial walnut desk in the corner between the windows.

An uncovered portable typewriter was on the desk, and a box of heavy, square notepaper with envelopes to match stood beside it. On the right-hand side of the typewriter there was a large glass ash tray with a dozen or more cigarette butts inside.

An envelope lying beyond the typewriter caught the detective's eye. It was from a newspaper-clipping service and addressed to Miss Wanda Weatherby. Shayne picked it up, opened it, and found a clipping inside with a printed slip pasted to the top with the name of the service and the typed information that it was from a Nashville paper, dated two weeks ago.

Shayne unfolded the clipping for a quick look. There was a picture of a woman and a young girl, both smiling happily into the camera. The caption read:

MRS. J. PIERSON GURLEY AND
DAUGHTER, JANET, OF MIAMI, FLORIDA

Shayne frowned as he glanced through the society item and read that Mrs. Gurley and her debutante daughter, prominent in Miami society, were guests at the Nashville home of Janet's fiancé, Thomas Marsh, III, making final plans for the wedding which would take place in Miami two months hence.

His frown deepened as he refolded the clipping and put it back in the envelope.

J. Pierson Gurley, prominent member of Miami's society, was actually Jack-The-Lantern Gurley.

It was quite true that he was well known in Miami's social circle, but in a different way from that implied by the clipping. Shayne itched to go through the drawers of the desk to see what else he might turn up, but he knew there wouldn't be time for that. He slid the envelope into his pocket and opened the door to the bathroom connecting the two rooms.

The bathroom was surprisingly large and beautifully appointed for a small bungalow. The sunken tub was fully six feet long, and there was a curtained dressing-alcove, and mirrors reflected his image everywhere. He didn't have time for an inventory, but Shayne was impressed by the cleanliness and the luxury of expensive taste, from the silver-topped cosmetic jars, the huge fluffy towels monogrammed *WW*, and other appointments that didn't quite fit into the pattern of disorder in the back bedroom where Wanda Weatherby apparently conducted whatever business she was engaged in.

The front bedroom confirmed his impression that the dead woman had done herself exceedingly well. The bed was an oversize Hollywood creation with a silk coverlet that touched the floor on both sides. The chests of drawers were large and seemed to be genuine antiques, and here, as in the bathroom, mirrors reflected the room from all available wall space. A chaise longue near the bed looked daintily feminine, covered in creamy silk to match the drapes and dotted with a pattern of blue flowers.

He heard a prowl car squealing to a stop as he opened the door of a large corner closet for a quick look. The smell of some exotic perfume floated out, and there was a neat array of dresses on padded hangers.

There was not the slightest sign anywhere of male occupancy, Shayne thought. He crossed the thick white rug to open the front door when he heard hurried footsteps approaching.

One of the uniformed men recognized Shayne. "Mike," he exclaimed. "We got a flash."

"I called in. She's in there," he said soberly. "I took a quick look around after I phoned," he went on, "but didn't make a thorough search. You want me outside?"

"Yeh, sure. Homicide'll be here, and then—"

"I'll stick around." He stepped aside and gestured toward the open door of the living-room. The patrolman entered, and Shayne went out past two officers stationed at the front door. He lit a cigarette, and drew smoke deeply into his lungs.

Other official cars began racing up at top speed, and brakes screeched. The lights went on in two of the neighboring houses, and curious faces appeared at windows.

Detective Dickerson, in charge of the first detail, leaped from his car and approached Shayne. He was a tall, slender man with incredibly wide shoulders. He said quietly, "What's the trouble here, Mike?"

"Murder," Shayne told him grimly. "I found her dead on the floor at ten thirty-eight. When she didn't answer her doorbell, I broke in the back door for a look. Then

I phoned in." He paused, taking another drag on his cigarette. "Have your men check the lawn from the first side window of the living-room to the hedge. Looks to me as though she was shot through the screen. Rifle, probably."

"Okay, Mike." Dickerson didn't ask any other questions, but said, "Stick around. Chief Gentry is on his way."

"I'll wait around." Shayne tossed his cigarette away and walked out on the lush green lawn, his hands deep in his trouser pockets.

The setup in Wanda Weatherby's house disturbed him. The contrast between the bare, dingy back bedroom and the rest of the house, so neat and clean and expensively furnished!

"Hello, Mike," a deep, rumbling voice interrupted his thoughts.

Shayne whirled around. "Oh, hello, Will."

Chief Will Gentry was a big, solid man with graying hair and slightly protuberant eyes the color of granite. He was chewing on the stub of a cigar which he tossed away before he asked, "What're you doing here, Mike?"

"When did you start chasing ambulances?"

"When they told me *you* called headquarters," he rumbled. "Who's the dame?"

"My guess is Wanda Weatherby. But you'll have to get somebody else to identify the body."

Gentry reached a pudgy hand to his hat and thrust it back from his forehead, rolled his crinkled lids up to study Shayne's face shrewdly in the faint moonlight. "Tell me about it."

"At ten o'clock tonight a woman called me. Said her name was Wanda Weatherby. I didn't know her, but she said she'd tried to call me twice today at my office and couldn't get me. She said she'd written me a letter I'd get in the morning. She was frightened and talked fast and didn't give me a chance to say no. She begged me to come out right away, and hung up. I tried to find her number and call her back, but she isn't listed in the telephone book. So I beat it out here. The house was lighted just as it is now, but she didn't answer when I rang. I took a gander through the side window there and saw her on the floor. I broke in the kitchen door. It was locked and I had to break the glass. When I saw she was dead and I couldn't help her, I phoned headquarters." He spread out his hands and added, "That's all."

Chief Gentry said stolidly, "Let's go in."

They walked across the lawn in silence and through the open doorway. A police doctor was bending over the body, photographers were snapping pictures of the death room, and other experts were prowling about the house, searching for physical clues.

Detective Dickerson met them just inside, holding the small lump of metal in his hand. "A soft-nosed bullet from a high-power rifle," he told the chief. "It was on the rug, about three feet from the body. Came through that open window across the room."

Shayne went past them to peer over the doctor's shoulder at the dead woman. The body had been turned over, and there was a small round hole just above the bridge of her nose where the bullet had entered. There was a trickle of blood from the hole, but otherwise her face was not disfigured.

She appeared to be in her early thirties, with smooth skin and carefully arched brows. The features were a trifle thin, nose and chin sharply outlined, and in life she probably possessed a serene and patrician beauty. In death, the face was pinched and tight, the jaw hanging laxly open and the inner portion of the lips showing blue beyond the line of crimson lipstick.

The police doctor rocked back on his heels and looked up as Gentry joined them. Then he came to his feet, yawned, and said, "They can take her away any time. Death was instantaneous and probably about an hour ago."

Gentry asked Shayne, "What time did you say she called you, Mike?"

"A few minutes after ten." His watch showed 10:53 now, and he nodded slowly. "That fits. She must have got it very soon after she hung up. Dickerson got anything else, Will?"

"Not much. A neighbor has identified her as Mrs. Weatherby. They're working the neighborhood for someone who heard the shot or saw anything.

"She rented this place about six months ago," the chief rumbled on. "Lives here alone. Has a cleaning woman come in every afternoon. Very unneighborly and reputed to have lots of money, and suspected of leading a gay life, but nothing definite. Now you give us something, Mike."

"I told you I had this phone call from her at ten o'clock."

"Was she terribly frightened?" Dickerson broke in. "As though she feared this?" he added, indicating the corpse.

"She was afraid, all right. Worked up and highly emotional. But I didn't get the impression she knew a murderer was waiting outside to shoot her. In other words, she had no reason to believe she wouldn't be alive to talk to me when I got here. At least, that's my impression," Shayne ended truthfully.

"What did she call you about today?" Gentry demanded.

"I have no idea. I was at the races and didn't get back

to the office. I can call Lucy and ask her."

"*I'll* call Lucy," said Gentry. "I've got one hell of a hunch you're holding out something, Mike. It smells like one of your stunts, damn it."

Shayne shrugged elaborately and lit a cigarette while Chief Gentry went to the phone to dial Lucy Hamilton's number.

He wasn't ready, yet, to tell about the telephone calls that had preceded Wanda's, and he didn't want company when he went to discuss Wanda with Rourke and his friend, Ralph Flannagan. That might come later, but right now he was in the middle of something without the slightest idea how he'd gotten there. Until he learned more about Wanda Weatherby and why she wanted to see him it was quite possible that he would be violating the confidence of a prospective client by giving information to the authorities about those three calls.

He listened with interest while Will Gentry spoke into the telephone. "That you, Lucy? Will Gentry. Sorry to bother you, but is Mike there?"

Gentry listened a moment, then rumbled placatingly, "No, I'm not taking over the morals squad. And it's not that late, anyhow. No reason Mike mightn't have stopped in for a drink. When did you see him last?"

He listened again, then explained. "It's about a woman who is supposed to have called his office this afternoon. Wanda Weatherby. Do you know if Mike talked to her?"

He listened for another interval, then said, "Okay, Lucy. If you hear from Mike ask him to check with me."

Shayne was grinning widely when he hung up.

Gentry said sourly, "You've got Lucy well trained or else you're telling the truth for once. She says this Weatherby woman called at two and again at four-thirty.

Wouldn't say what she wanted except that it was personal, and she sounded worried. The last time, she told Lucy she was writing you a letter and mailing it."

"You want to search me for a thirty-caliber rifle before I go?" Shayne asked. "I guess my time of arrival could fit, couldn't it, Doc?"

The doctor was closing his bag. "Anywhere from half an hour to an hour and a half."

Will Gentry made an impatient gesture. His ruddy and normally pleasant face wore a scowl. "Quit horsing around, Mike. I'll be at your office when the mail arrives in the morning."

Shayne said, "Fine. And I'll show you Wanda's letter if I feel like it." He turned and strode out, angry with himself for having been jockeyed into a position at cross-purposes with Gentry, yet stubbornly certain that he had a much better chance of turning up the truth about Wanda's death if he went at it his own way without interference from the police.

Jack Gurley's Sportsman's Club was located on the shore of Biscayne Bay in the Sixties. Shayne pondered over the clipping in his pocket as he drove swiftly to the club. He knew Gurley slightly and, in a sense, respected the man. "The Lantern" had been one of Capone's minor mobsters in prohibition days, and had parlayed a fast trigger and cold-blooded disdain for human life into a small fortune and a position of semirespectability in the course of twenty years.

His Sportsman's Club was actually a club—with a membership strictly limited to men who were in the big money and enjoyed spending it lavishly. The annual dues paid by each member were rumored to be five thousand dollars, but for this sum free food and liquor were available at

the club twenty-four hours a day every day in the year.
Admittance was by card only, but guests of members were
welcomed at a modest assessment of one hundred dollars
a day, billed to his host at the end of the month. Since it
was a private club and, strictly speaking, he sold no food
or liquor on the premises, Gurley was not hampered by
licensing-restrictions or closing-hours. If his sporting members and their guests enjoyed gambling, it was available
to them on the second floor in luxurious surroundings,
also on a twenty-four-hour basis and with a monthly set-
tlement of wins and losses which made the losing of money
just about as painless as possible.

Shayne had never been inside the club, since he had no
intimate friends who were eager to press a hundred-dollar-
a-day guest card on him. It was a large, three-story wooden
building directly at the dead end of a street, with a large
parking-lot on each side, and a modest canopied entrance
with an alert young man to open the door of one's car
and drive it away for him.

The attendant was waiting when Shayne drove to the
club and braked his car. Shayne got out, gave his name,
and said, "Spot it close. I only expect to be here a few
minutes."

The young man said, "Certainly, Mr. Shayne."

The detective walked up beneath the canopy where a
suave individual wearing a dinner jacket bowed and said
quietly, "Your card, sir?"

Shayne said, "I haven't any card. Send word to Jack
Gurley that I'm here. Michael Shayne. It's business."

"I'm not sure that Mr. Gurley will be immediately
available, sir. If you'd care to wait here—"

"I'll wait, but tell him to make it fast."

The man nodded and went to speak to a confrere who

stood beside glass doors that opened into a cocktail lounge.

There were maroon-covered settees in the small ante-room. Shayne sat down and stretched out his long legs to wait.

As he had anticipated, the wait was short. He hadn't quite finished his first cigarette when another clean-cut young man, much like the one who had taken his car, appeared unobtrusively from a side door leading off the anteroom. He said, "Mr. Shayne? This way, please."

Shayne followed him through the door and up a carpeted stairway to a door on the third floor. It stood open, and he entered a large, simply furnished office.

He faced the owner of the club across a wide gleaming expanse of clean mahogany desk. Gurley wore a loose tweed suit and a soft white shirt. He had a square, impassive face, with tufted gray brows and short black hair sprinkled with gray. His big hands were folded on the desk, and he surveyed Shayne with interest, but without friendliness. He had gotten his nickname of The Lantern from a complaint made early in his career as proprietor of the Sportsman's Club that it was impossible to find honest men for his gambling-tables.

"If you're looking for a job, shamus," Gurley said with a faintly derisive smile, "I can use a head bouncer."

Shayne tossed his hat on the desk and pulled up a chair to face Gurley. He said casually, "Still carrying the lantern, eh?"

"Still carrying it. I'll blow it out if you go to work for me."

Shayne grinned and shook his head. "I'd rather stay honest. What I dropped in about was to ask you what the hell you meant by having one of your goons bother me with that telephone call this evening."

CHAPTER FOUR

J. PIERSON GURLEY unfolded his fingers and carefully placed the tips of them together. He said pleasantly, "Get up to date, Shayne. I graduated from the goon period in my life. I'm a legitimate businessman now."

"They're still goons to me, no matter if you call them vice-presidents," Shayne told him evenly. "And I don't like anonymous threats over the telephone."

"You want a thing done right," said Gurley with a sigh, "do it yourself." He opened a drawer and took out a sandalwood box of cigars and offered one to Shayne.

Shayne declined the offer, and got out a pack of cigarettes.

Gurley took a cigar and bit off the end with strong teeth. He asked wearily, "Why come to me about some telephone call?"

"Because I like to do my talking to the top guy."

"What makes you think I'm the top?"

"Stop batting it around," said Shayne impatiently. "It was a fool move, trying to warn me off Wanda Weatherby. A legitimate businessman ought to know better."

"Have you talked to Wanda?" demanded Gurley.

Shayne said, "No."

"Don't." Gurley drew a silver table lighter toward him and put the flame to the cigar. "And if you're smart you'll tear up that letter without reading it."

"Sometimes I guess I'm not very smart."

"How right you are. I can have you run out of Miami,

shamus."

"I doubt that."

"Or carried out feet first."

"I doubt that, too." Anger blazed in Shayne's gray eyes. He leaned forward and doubled one hand into a fist. "Do you want to talk about Wanda Weatherby before I read her letter—or afterward?"

Gurley said, "You're making a big mistake."

"Nuts to that!" Shayne shoved his chair back and stood up, leaning over the desk with both hands flat on the desk. "You and your cheap trigger boys. Keep them off my tail, Gurley. If any of them mess with me, I'll hold you accountable."

Jack-The-Lantern Gurley leaned back comfortably and clasped both hands behind his head. "Sounds to me," he drawled, "as though you've been reading some of your own publicity. Get wise to yourself and don't let the Weatherby bitch suck you into anything. If I hadn't thought you knew how to add two and two I'd never bothered tipping you off. If you want money," he added indifferently, "I'll pay you five times what she offers."

"She hasn't offered me anything yet."

"There'll be a grand in her letter tomorrow. Mail it back to her and the next morning there'll be an envelope with five thousand in it."

"In payment for what?"

"For not snooping into things that don't concern you. Look," the club proprietor continued persuasively, "we're both businessmen. So we make a deal. I admit it was probably a mistake to have Nick telephone you. But hell! I don't know you very well. I can see now that you're a lot like me. I'd get sore, too, and stick my neck out if I was given the office to lay off. So you didn't scare. Okay. It would have been cheaper if you had, so you can't blame me for trying."

"What has she got on you?" Shayne demanded.

"Nothing," said Gurley promptly. "But I don't like stinks. Somebody," he added darkly, "is going to bump that dame off some day, and I don't want to be involved. That's all. You know how it is when a man's name gets mixed up in a murder investigation."

"Yeh. I know. That's why I came for your side of it first," Shayne stated flatly. He paused, holding his breath to see whether Gurley would rise to the bait. If he had ordered the rifle shot that sent a bullet into Wanda's brain, he must realize that she was already dead. And that was the only way he could possibly know so soon.

But the gambler either didn't know or was too smart to fall into the trap. He said casually, "I've got nothing to tell anybody about Wanda Weatherby. And you can make five grand in one day—and stay healthy on top of that by staying clear of that dame."

Michael Shayne jerked himself erect and picked up his hat from the desk. He said, "I hear your daughter is being married soon. Congratulations."

"What does that crack mean?" Gurley stiffened and his voice was abruptly cold with anger.

Shayne shrugged. "Is it a crack to congratulate a girl's father on hooking a husband like Thomas Marsh the Third; of the Nashville Marshes, isn't he?"

He knew he had struck pay dirt by the expression on Gurley's normally impassive features. But all the gambler said was, "Get out, Shayne."

"Sure. I don't like stinks, either." He turned and walked out deliberately, went down the stairs and into the small anteroom.

The doorman said, "I'll have your car for you at once, Mr. Shayne." He turned and spoke into the mouthpiece of an intercommunication set.

Shayne brushed past him and went out the door where he strode to the end of the canopy and waited. He knew he had been a fool to lose his temper with Jack-The-Lantern Gurley. That wasn't the right approach to a man like that. And he hadn't learned anything except that his hunch as to the source of the mysterious telephone call had been correct.

There was still Timothy Rourke's friend on Fortieth Street. And a woman named Sheila Martin who had promised to see him at twelve. Between them, he might be able to learn something about Wanda Weatherby and why she had been murdered.

CHAPTER FIVE

THE COURTLAND ARMS was located on East Fortieth Street, one of the newer and larger apartment houses in the city. A severely utilitarian building with the entrance near the sidewalk. The lobby was small, equipped with a long, narrow table centered by a tall potted plant, and two large ash trays; there were three leather chairs, an information desk on the left, and a switchboard behind it.

An elegant white-haired lady sat at the switchboard. She turned to look Shayne over with impersonal disinterest as he approached.

He said, "Flannagan? Number twenty-six, I believe."

"Yes. Is Mr. Flannagan expecting you?"

Shayne said he was, and she told him that the apartment was on the second floor to the right of the elevator.

The cage was waiting on the ground floor, and the detective tramped over, pushed the button to open the door, and went up. He pressed the button of Apartment 26, and the door was opened almost immediately.

Ralph Flannagan said, "Mr. Shayne? Come right in. My God, am I glad to see you!"

His hand was well-fleshed, but his grip was hard, and he wrung Shayne's with an effusive heartiness that seemed a trifle out of place under the circumstances.

In fact, the immediate and over-all impression conveyed by Flannagan was that he was working hard at being hearty and masculine and vital. His heavy black hair was cut too short, and his features were plump; his body thick and stocky. He gripped a bulldog pipe between his teeth, and managed to look tweedy and outdoorish, though he wore a shabby smoking-jacket over a white shirt with the two buttons open to reveal a tanned and hairy neck. Walking behind him as he led the way through the small foyer, Shayne noted that his rump was exceedingly fat, and it jiggled with each step.

Through the archway, and over Flannagan's head, Shayne saw Timothy Rourke's emaciated body sprawled in a deep chair. He had a highball glass in his right hand. On his left, atop an end table, a deep ash tray was heaped with cigarette butts.

The reporter raised his glass and said, "Hi," as his host hustled the detective through the archway into the living-room. Low bookshelves along one wall were crammed with much-handled volumes, and an imposing radio-phonograph combination was flanked by two tall, well-filled record cabinets. The couch and three comfortable chairs were covered with maroon slipcovers, and all were equipped with convenient end tables and ash trays. A room where a man could relax with smokes and drinks and good books.

But, he thought wryly, it was a little too much for the room. It was as though the effect had been carefully calculated instead of merely accumulative through the normal course of living. As though the occupant was aggressively determined to prove himself the sort of man who *would* have such a room. A tenuous impression, he told himself, and probably unfair to Ralph Flannagan.

"Hi, Tim," Shayne greeted Rourke. He grinned widely and added, "The body looks natural—with a tall glass in one hand."

"Have a seat, Mr. Shayne," Flannagan said. "Make yourself comfortable. I don't have to ask what you'd like to drink," he went on effusively. "Cognac, eh?" His white teeth flashed in a smile that would have been a simper on a less masculine face.

"About three fingers in a washtub," Shayne told him. "With a glass of ice water on the side. I see that my reputation has preceded my visit," he added, glancing at Rourke.

Flannagan chuckled and went toward the kitchen. Shayne's gaze followed him, curiously, until he disappeared through a door at the far end of the room.

Timothy Rourke said lazily, "Don't blame Ralph for being a little edgy and determined to please. He's really up against a tough problem, and he figures you're the only man in Miami who can help him."

Shayne was still standing, looking around. He shrugged, noncommittal, and turned to look at the bookshelf. Three brightly jacketed modern novels attracted his attention, along with a much-thumbed copy of Guyon's *The Ethics of Sexual Acts*, two novels by Arnold Bennett, *The New Way to Eat and Get Slim* which didn't appear to have had hard usage, and a bulky three-volume set of *The Reminiscences of Carl Schurz*.

Flannagan returned with a tray holding a full bottle of Martell and an empty four-ounce glass, some ice water, and a highball glass with just enough Scotch to faintly color the contents.

Shayne sat down on the couch, and his host set the tray on the small table at his right, remarking, "You see, I've heard and read a lot about you, Mr. Shayne, and know just how you like things." He lifted the highball off for himself and sat down.

"Thanks," said Shayne. He turned to Timothy Rourke

and asked, "What was it you wanted to tell me about Wanda Weatherby, Tim?"

"It's Ralph's story."

"Let's have it," Shayne suggested. He poured cognac in his glass, took a long drink, and chased it with ice water.

"By all means," said Ralph Flannagan eagerly. Seated in his favorite chair, he stuffed tobacco in the bowl of his big pipe. "I'm going to be completely frank with you, Mr. Shayne. I know your reputation, and I know you're a good friend of Tim's. I have a feeling you'll understand and won't let me down."

Shayne didn't say anything. He took a drink of Martell and chased it with ice water.

"It goes back to a party about three months ago," Flannagan began. "The first time I met Wanda. It was at a friend's place over on the Beach. One of those informal, Bohemian affairs where people drift in and out for drinks and talk after dinner."

He paused, puffed vigorously on his pipe for a moment, then resumed. "I don't know how to describe Wanda. She wasn't beautiful, but there was something that hit a man right in the solar plexus when she looked at him. Something that came from deep within her, and was honest and strong." He shrugged his thick shoulders and stared down at the door. "Call it sex appeal, if you like. We looked at each other across the crowded room—and there it was. Pulsing between us so you could feel it—so it was almost material. We hadn't been introduced, but I remember crossing the room to her and holding out my hands."

"Save the harrowing details of the seduction for your radio audience," Rourke advised dryly. To Shayne he added, "Ralph writes and produces a daily radio serial for frustrated housewives, so don't blame him too much for clichés. They're his living."

Flannagan smiled patiently and said, "It was hardly a seduction, Tim. God knows I had no thought of anything like that when I sat down beside Wanda and we introduced ourselves. I was engaged to Edna, and as much in love with her as a man can be. But this was different. It was something outside ourselves. Something that was meant to be. We both had quite a few drinks, of course."

He paused again, then went on in an honest and man-to-man way. "I won't say it was she who made the advances, though I will say she did her part to make things easy. I told her about Edna. I was very careful to explain that I was deeply in love with a wonderful girl for the first time in my life, and she understood perfectly. She told me she was married and in love with her husband, and suggested that the thing between us had nothing to do with love or with any other aspect of our individual lives."

Shayne broke in sarcastically, "Okay. It has happened before. Then what?"

Flannagan frowned. "I'm telling you how it happened," he protested, "so you won't get any wrong ideas about Wanda. She was perfectly marvelous all the way through, and that's why I don't understand—well— But I'll come to that later. We did break away from the party, and there was mutual understanding as we went out to my car. No questions and no coyness. I suggested coming here to my apartment, but she vetoed that. Said it put things on too personal a basis, and she'd feel she was intruding on my private life. She wanted it completely impersonal. Just a beautiful experience that we could hold in our memories forever. A meeting, a mingling, and separation."

Shayne settled back more comfortably and emptied his cognac glass. It was easy to understand why Flannagan was a success at producing a radio serial. The man probably took himself seriously—actually believed the platitudes that were mouthed over the microphone every day. He was under thirty, Shayne guessed. Flannagan's voice flowed on smoothly, and the detective listened while he refilled his glass, seeing Wanda Weatherby's face in death as Ralph's story brought her to life for him.

"She suggested a motel as being most discreet," he was saying, "and we drove out the Boulevard to a nice one on the outskirts of the city. I registered as Mr. and Mrs. Albert Smith and we were assigned to a clean, attractive cabin. I got a bottle from a near-by liquor store, and some ice and glasses from the motel manager, and we had a few more drinks." He stopped, reddening a little, and knocked out his dead pipe in an ash tray.

"I suppose this part won't bother you much, Mr. Shayne, being a private detective, but the thing that happened was horrible. Absolutely horrible. I never felt so sickened and cheapened in my life."

Flannagan drew in a deep breath, set his jaw, and went on rapidly. "I was just getting up when the cabin door opened. I could have sworn I'd locked it securely, but I guess I hadn't. Naturally I turned to see who was coming in. Then, a sudden brilliant flare burst in my eyes, half blinding me, but I saw a man with a camera. He slammed the door and ran, and we heard a car pulling away in a hurry.

"Wanda was terribly frightened and upset, and— Well, I was, too, to admit the truth. Everything was ruined. The whole affair was suddenly dirty and vicious. Neither of us could understand how on earth anybody had followed us, or why. It was simply inconceivable, but there it was. We drove back to town fast, sobered and ashamed and without talking much.

"What was there to say?" the radio producer continued. "She made me let her out on the Boulevard and wouldn't even tell me where she lived. It was over—and we both knew the golden moment would never come again. Not for us. There would always be that nasty memory between us."

"Did she make a telephone call," Shayne demanded, "after you registered at the motel?"

"Why—yes. While I went for the bottle of liquor. You see, she was living here with her husband's sister and had to call her to give an explanation for not coming home from the party until quite late."

"Maybe," Shayne said curtly. "And maybe that phone was made to an accomplice with a camera. It happens every day in Miami."

"No—you're absolutely wrong, Mr. Shayne," said Flannagan flatly. "I confess thinking something of the sort after—what happened. But I learned the truth later. It was her husband, you see. He's a businessman in Detroit and insanely jealous. When Wanda came down here to visit his sister, he had a private detective watching her. She told me about it a week later. This detective had come to her with the evidence. He had the picture and a Photostat of my signature on the motel register. He was one of the unethical members of your profession, Mr. Shayne, and was quite willing to sell out his employer for a price. He offered Wanda the evidence against her for a thousand dollars."

"What was his name?" asked Shayne.

"She didn't tell me. In fact, I doubt if she knew herself.

She was terrified, of course, both for herself and for me. There was my engagement to Edna and her marriage both at stake. She felt exceedingly guilty about getting me into such a mess, and was very decent about the whole thing, I thought. She insisted on paying half the money if I would pay the other half. I wanted to pay the whole thing, but she wouldn't hear of it."

Shayne said, "So you got the picture and Photostat back and felt damned lucky to get out of it for only five hundred."

"I gave her the money and she got them back. Yes. She called me two days later to say it was all right and I had nothing to worry about. I didn't hear from her again for almost a month."

Ralph Flannagan got up abruptly and began to pace up and down the room, thumping the bowl of his pipe into the palm of his left hand. His brow was corrugated.

"She telephoned to say she was going to have a baby. I met her in a bar and we talked it over. She had been to a doctor and there wasn't any doubt. And she hadn't seen her husband for more than two months. It was a terrible mess. Even then she was wonderful and courageous about it," he went on doggedly. "After learning what a swine her husband was in having a detective follow her, she was determined not to go back to him. She was equally determined not to break up my life, either. She wanted nothing at all from me except some help to support herself until the baby came, and until she was well enough to support herself.

"I felt like a complete heel about it," he went on huskily. "I offered to break my engagement with Edna and marry her at once. She wouldn't even consider it. She said quite calmly that it was as much her fault as mine, and that my life mustn't be ruined by that one moment of giving way to madness.

"And she was completely reasonable and realistic about the financial arrangements, too." He chewed on the stem of his pipe, and his face was gloomy. "Sometimes I think women are a lot more realistic than men about such things. We didn't love each other, she pointed out, and it would be foolish for me to throw everything up and marry her just to be quixotic. She had learned more about Edna by then, and insisted that I go right ahead with our wedding plans next month." He sank heavily into his chair and sighed.

"What Ralph has neglected to explain," Tim Rourke said into the brief silence, "is that his fiancée is the daughter of the guy who sponsors his radio program. To put it crudely, Wanda preferred a steady income to a husband who couldn't support her."

"That was only part of it," said Ralph with dignity. "We did discuss that aspect. Why not? I admitted I'd likely lose my program sponsorship if the truth came out, or if I jilted Edna without a good explanation. After all, that wouldn't have made things easier. Keeping things as they were meant that I could earn enough so I could afford to give Wanda what she needed. And why shouldn't she have security at such a time?"

"How much?" Shayne asked.

"How much do I earn?"

"How much did she want?"

"Oh. A hundred a week. You see, she had to move away from her sister-in-law's and get a place of her own where she wasn't known."

"And you paid her that?" Shayne queried.

"Of course I did. What else could any decent man do?

I was glad to. It was definitely my responsibility." Flannagan leaned forward and thrust his jaw out pugnaciously, as though challenging Shayne to disagree.

Shayne nodded and said mildly, "What's the latest development?"

"That's what I simply cannot understand." Flannagan twisted his pipe around and around in his big, boyish hands.

"I was working here on a script about six o'clock, and expecting some actors in to audition for some new parts in my show. A messenger brought me a letter. Show it to him, Tim."

Timothy Rourke took a square white envelope from his pocket and handed it to the detective. Then he got up and asked, "Mind if I mix myself another slug, Ralph?"

"Of course not. You know where things are." The producer was watching Shayne anxiously. "When you read the enclosure you'll understand what a thunderbolt it was to me and why I called Tim Rourke to come over."

The envelope was addressed to Ralph Flannagan on a typewriter with elite type. There was no return address. Shayne took out the single sheet of plain white notepaper and found a carbon copy of a letter addressed to him:

Dear Mr. Shayne:

   I tried to call you at your office twice today, but you were out, and now it's five o'clock and I suppose I can't reach you tonight. So I'm going to put this in the mail with $1000 as a retainer and if anything does happen to me tonight you'll know that Ralph Flannagan, Apt. No. 26, the Courtland Arms, is guilty. The $1000 will be your fee for convicting him of my murder. He has tried to murder me twice in the last week and I'm desperately afraid *he is getting ready to try again.*

I am going to send Ralph a carbon of this letter by special messenger so he'll know there's no use his doing it tonight, hoping he'll go unsuspected. It's the only way I see to protect myself until I can talk to you.

I will telephone you for an appointment first thing in the morning if I'm alive.

The signature, *Wanda Weatherby*, was typed on the carbon.

Rourke sauntered back from the kitchen with a fresh drink and resumed his sprawled position as Shayne laid the letter aside.

Flannagan said rapidly and in an anguished voice, "You can see how I felt when I read what Wanda had written to you. My God! I didn't know what to think. I thought she had suddenly gone mad. Everything had been perfectly straight between us. I've sent her a hundred every week. And I certainly have *not* threatened her—or had any notion of doing so."

"She says here," Shayne reminded him, "that you've tried to kill her twice in the last week."

"It's fantastic! I haven't seen her or had any communication with her for over a month. If anyone tried to harm her, it certainly was not me. Do you think she's suddenly gone crazy, Mr. Shayne? Some sort of persecution complex? I've heard that some women act funny and get all sorts of ideas when they're pregnant."

Shayne said, "Her letter sounds quite sane—well reasoned out." He paused, recalling Wanda's voice as she had spoken to him over the telephone such a brief time before she died. Highly emotional, yes, but sensible enough. And the bullet in her head was proof enough that she had sufficient reason to fear for her life.

He said to Flannagan, "You got this by messenger about six o'clock. What did you do?"

"First I tried to telephone her. She has an unlisted number, and it didn't answer. Then I recalled the name of your hotel and tried to call you. But you were out. I didn't know what to do. Then I called Tim Rourke. That was about seven o'clock, I guess." He glanced inquiringly at the reporter.

Rourke nodded. "A little after seven," he told Shayne. "Ralph gave me an idea of what was up, and I agreed to come over and read the letter and maybe help him get hold of you."

"I had some important audition appointments," the producer went on, "and asked Tim if he could come about a quarter of ten. I thought if I could get in touch with you and explain things before you opened that letter from Wanda in the morning, you might be willing to help me by finding out what in hell she meant without dragging my name in," he ended unhappily.

"What time did you get here?" Shayne asked Rourke.

"About ten of ten. I was only a few minutes late. Ralph was just finishing a shower, and he gave me the letter to read. We talked it over briefly. Then I called you."

"About five after ten," the detective agreed. "What did you do then?"

"We sat here and talked about life and Wanda Weatherby," the reporter told him with a grin. "And had a few drinks and waited for you to show up."

"Can you swear that Flannagan was right here from ten o'clock on?" Shayne asked. "He didn't go out to mail a letter—or for any reason?"

"No. He was right here with me. Biting his nails down

to the quick and waiting for you."

Shayne picked up the carbon copy of Wanda's letter and tapped it against his knuckles. "I wouldn't worry about this too much," he told Ralph Flannagan somberly. "Someone did you a big favor by disposing of Wanda Weatherby between ten and ten-thirty tonight—during the time that Tim swears you were here with him."

CHAPTER SIX

BOTH MEN SAT VERY STILL and stared at Shayne for a long moment. Then Ralph Flannagan said in a hoarse whisper, "Disposed of her? Do you mean—"

"With a rifle bullet through her head," Shayne stated in a flat voice. "She called me at ten o'clock—and was dead when I arrived at her house on Seventy-Fifth Street."

The radio producer shuddered and buried his face in his hands and moaned, "Wanda."

Rourke dragged his thin body up and leaned toward Shayne, his cavernous, slate-gray eyes feverish with interest. "Then she *had* picked the wrong guy to be afraid of. Any other dope, Mike?"

"Nothing. She probably didn't see her killer. He stood outside and fired through the wire screen."

"To prevent her from talking to you?"

"It's a fair inference," Shayne told him with a shrug. "It's even possible he was standing close enough to the open window to have overheard her call. If he knew about this letter she had written me accusing Flannagan, it would have seemed a perfect time to bump her and hope that you would be the fall guy, Flannagan."

"Which I might have been so easily," the producer muttered, lifting his head and shaking it distraughtly. "If I didn't have an alibi. If Tim hadn't happened to be here at the right time."

"Who else did you tell about the letter?" Shayne demanded.

"Why—no one," he protested in a shocked voice. "My God! It isn't the sort of thing a man would discuss."

"You said some people came in for auditions," Shayne pressed him. "Are you sure you didn't mention it?"

"Positive," said Flannagan.

"How many people knew about your affair with Wanda? And that you were paying her blackmail?"

Flannagan's face suffused with anger and his heavy jaw jutted. "It wasn't blackmail at all. I won't let you think that about Wanda. It was I who insisted on paying her the money."

"Nevertheless," Shayne pointed out grimly, "it's a hell of a good motive for murder—on the surface. Here you are, engaged to a wealthy girl, with your livelihood at stake if your affair with Wanda comes out. What I'm trying to point out is that anyone who knew the truth about you, and who had some personal reason for wanting Wanda out of the way would know you'd be the prime suspect if anything happened to her. Look at her letter," he went on. "No matter how you felt about the affair, Wanda herself suspected you of planning to kill her. She accuses you of having made two previous attempts. How many people knew the truth?"

"No one. I swear I never told anyone. Good heavens! If a word of it had leaked out—" He broke off, shuddering at the thought.

"Do you know a man named Gurley?" Shayne asked abruptly.

Flannagan frowned, then said, "I don't—think so."

"Jack Pierson Gurley," Shayne amplified, "sometimes known as Jack-The-Lantern."

"Oh, that one? I've heard about him and his swanky gambling-club, but I've never met him personally."

"Ever hear Wanda mention his name?"

"I don't think so. I've explained that we weren't actually intimate. That is, I honestly don't know much about her personal life. We only met briefly those few times."

"Think back on those few times and concentrate," growled Shayne. "Can you remember anything at all to indicate a connection between her and Jack Gurley—or the Sportsman's Club?"

The producer shook his head helplessly. "Not a thing, I'm afraid."

"What's this about Gurley?" Rourke asked eagerly.

"I don't know. There's some connection, all right." Shayne hesitated, thinking back over his talk with the gambler.

Gurley was one person who knew about the letter Wanda had written accusing Flannagan of planning her death. He had known about the letter even before her death, as evidenced by the first telephone call by one of his goons earlier in the evening. But why the devil should Gurley be so anxious to have the letter destroyed unread? What was his interest in Ralph Flannagan? If Gurley had ordered her death because she had pointed the finger at Flannagan, he certainly wouldn't want the letter destroyed.

Unless, of course, he had some personal reason for wanting to protect Flannagan from suspicion.

Shayne's brow was furrowed when he said harshly, "Don't lie to me, Flannagan. What about Gurley's daughter, Janet? How well do you know her?"

"I don't know Gurley and I didn't know he had a daughter," the radio producer told him. "So far as I can recall right now, I don't know any girl named Janet."

"What about a woman named Sheila Martin?"

Again Ralph Flannagan shook his head helplessly.

"That doesn't click, either. I've told you I didn't really *know* Wanda. I was never in her home. I've never met any of her friends or talked about her personal affairs."

"What about the party where you met her? Didn't anyone there know her?"

"Why—I suppose someone must have invited her. But I don't really know. I've explained the sort of party it was. She might have come with someone else who had been invited. You know how those parties are. I didn't see her talking to anyone. She was sitting alone when I noticed her, and we left together shortly afterward."

Shayne sighed and said, "All right. So we get back to the situation between the two of you and the fact that she suspected you of having tried to kill her twice and of planning another attempt. Who could have known you were responsible for her condition—and thus a logical suspect if she were killed?"

"I swear I have not told anyone. Do you mean you think perhaps Wanda didn't actually write that letter to me?" His face lit up hopefully. "That must be it. I just can't believe Wanda felt that way about me. But who could have found out the truth?"

"Wanda knew," Shayne reminded him. "She might have told others. And there is the detective who took the picture of you and sold it back to her. There's no way of knowing whether a louse like that actually did sell it back to her or not," he went on disgustedly. "Having shaken her down for a grand, what was to prevent his going ahead and turning over a duplicate set to her husband to collect his fee?"

"Oh, no. I'm certain he didn't do that. Wanda told me he gave her the original Photostat and the negative—and that she destroyed them immediately."

"Photostats can be copied," Shayne reminded him wearily. "And a duplicate negative can easily be made from a print. The police will probably check pretty closely on her husband."

"What! You mean they'll have to—know all about this?" Flannagan faltered. "It will ruin me, Shayne! Can't you keep the information confidential? Work on the case yourself? If I'm your client, you don't have to tell them, do you? Isn't there something in the law about a private detective having the same right to refuse to divulge confidential information from a client as a lawyer?" The radio producer grew more excited as he spoke, leaning tensely toward the detective.

"There is that," Shayne agreed. "But as soon as I receive the original of this letter in the morning's mail with Wanda Weatherby's retainer, *she* will legally become my client."

"Can't we both be?" pleaded Flannagan. "I'll employ you on the same terms to do the same job. *I* want her murderer found, too."

"The way her letter reads," the detective reminded him gruffly, "the thousand dollars is being paid me to convict *you* of her murder."

There was a brief, heavy silence, then Timothy Rourke said, "You know you can't prove Ralph murdered her, Mike, because I can prove he didn't. It seems to me you're ethically bound to turn her retainer down. Hell, Mike. Give the guy a break. You can do more with information like this in solving the case than the police can," he continued persuasively. "Why drag Ralph through the mud when you know he's innocent?"

"I'm not eager to drag anybody through the mud," said Shayne angrily. "You've known me long enough to know that. It's just that my hands are practically tied on this thing. I don't see any chance of keeping the police out."

"You mean you told them about coming here to Ralph's place?"

"No. As a matter of fact, I didn't. Will Gentry was there and he rubbed me the wrong way by disbelieving me when I said I didn't know a damned thing about Wanda Weatherby except her telephone call."

"Why tell him now?" Rourke urged. "He'll just be sore because you didn't bring him along. Let Ralph pay you the retainer, if you want to get legal about it, and have an out for keeping this letter quiet."

"Please, Mr. Shayne," Flannagan broke in earnestly, "I'd want to help find Wanda's murderer, even if I weren't involved as a suspect. Let me give you a check for a thousand dollars right now." He had both hands on the arms of his chair, ready to spring up.

When Shayne hesitated, Rourke said in a cynical tone, "He can afford it, Mike. It only amounts to the next ten weekly payments that he won't have to pay Wanda now."

"I don't like to have you put it on that basis, Tim," Flannagan said swiftly and angrily. "You make it sound as though I'm glad Wanda is dead."

Shayne apparently ignored both of them. He said soberly, "Even if I don't turn this carbon over to the police, there's the original arriving in the mail tomorrow morning. Gentry knows about that, and he'll be waiting in my office to grab it when it's delivered."

"How did he know about it?" Flannagan asked.

"She told me about it over the telephone, and she also explained to my secretary that she was going to mail it when she called my office and couldn't get me." Shayne paused, then added, "Of course, Will Gentry has no idea what will be in her letter. Neither did I until I came here."

Again, the silence was heavy between them. Shayne tugged at his left earlobe and frowned thoughtfully. He glanced at his watch. The time was nearly midnight—and his appointment with Sheila Martin, from whom he hoped to learn more about Wanda Weatherby, was only a few minutes away. He drank his cognac and stood up, saying to his host, "May I use your telephone?"

Ralph Flannagan leaped to his feet. "Certainly. It's right in here." He led the way to open a door into a bedroom on the other side, switched on the light, and stepped aside, explaining, "I do all my homework here, so excuse the way things look. The telephone's right there on the desk."

Here was another long, narrow room, almost the length of the living-room. There was a double bed at one end, and built-in bookshelves on both sides, and a reading-light attached to the headboard. The other end of the bedroom was fitted up as an office with a large desk, and a standard model typewriter. There were neat stacks of typed scripts on the desk, and an oversize wastebasket beside the chair overflowed with crumpled sheets of paper.

The telephone was to the left of the typewriter and within easy reach. Beyond it stood a portable tape recorder equipped with a microphone that hung from a hook in the ceiling several feet from the desk and about five feet from the floor. On the right of the desk an open door revealed a bathroom with the lights on.

"It's not a very fancy boudoir," Flannagan apologized again as Shayne walked toward the desk, "but it's handy if I want to jump out of bed at any time in the night when an idea or a bit of dialogue comes to me."

Shayne glanced at the dangling microphone as he went

by, and commented, "If you had the mike hanging over the bed, you wouldn't even have to get up in the night."

"Oh, I never dictate my stuff," the producer assured him. "I'm conditioned to the typewriter. I use the microphone to record auditions and bits of rehearsal when I have some of my actors in."

"This is a personal call," Shayne said, and waited with his hand on the telephone. Flannagan flushed and immediately withdrew, closing the door firmly as he went out.

It was strange how the guy got on his nerves, Shayne thought wryly as he dialed Lucy Hamilton's number. There was nothing he could put his finger on, but somehow Ralph Flannagan rubbed him the wrong way.

Lucy's phone rang three times before she answered. Shayne asked, "Did I wake you?"

"Michael! No. I couldn't get to sleep after Chief Gentry called me a while ago. He wants you to call—"

"Yeh. I know," Shayne growled. "I was standing at his elbow when he went through that routine. Never mind that," he went on swiftly. "What sort of type do you have on your portable typewriter there in the apartment?"

"Elite. Why? What's up, Michael?" she asked anxiously. "Shouldn't I have told Gentry about those telephone calls?"

"That was okay," Shayne reassured her. "There's nothing much up right at the moment except that Wanda Weatherby is dead and Gentry and I both wonder why she wanted to see me. Go back to sleep if you can. I may have to drop in on you later, but don't wait up for me. What time does the first mail reach the office?"

"A little after nine, usually. If there's anything I can do—"

"If there is, I'll be seeing you. Good night."

He hung up and went back to the living-room where his anxious host jumped up and asked, "Did you fix—"

"I'm not positive I can do anything for you," Shayne told him soberly. "But you might write out that check for a thousand if you still want to. I won't cash it unless I find a way to keep your name out of the murder investigation."

"I want to thank you, Mr. Shayne. I'll be right back with the check, and—"

"Don't thank me yet," Shayne said.

Flannagan hurried away, and Shayne crossed over to Rourke's chair, scowled, and muttered, "When we get out of here, I want to know why you're so willing to pass up a juicy story."

Rourke said, "Okay," and got up to stretch his stiff limbs.

Flannagan returned, waving a check in the air to dry the ink. He handed it to the detective, who folded it and put it in his pocket.

"I think I'll go along with Mike, Ralph," said Rourke. "I'll be in touch with you, huh?"

"You bet," Flannagan returned genially. "And I can't ever thank you enough, Tim. And, Mr. Shayne, I don't know how to tell you how much—"

"Wait until I cash this check," Shayne advised. "And if I do cash it, an invitation to your wedding will be thanks enough." He picked up his hat and went out, waited a moment for Rourke, and they went down the corridor to the elevator together.

"Ralph isn't a bad guy, Mike," Rourke said as he stretched his thin legs to keep pace with the rangy detective. "I've known him a long time and he really had

talent when he went into radio work. Now, he's all mixed
up and frustrated on account of the drivel he has to write
to hang onto his job."

"His relation with Wanda Weatherby would make a
swell headline for tomorrow's paper," said Shayne shortly.
The elevator came up and they got in.

"But the guy's innocent, Mike," the reporter argued.
"Damn it— we *know* he is."

"Do you believe his version of the affair with Wanda?"

"Absolutely. From his viewpoint, at least. He's actually
that naïve, Mike. She could be the toughest little hooker
in Miami taking Ralph for a ride all the way, but he'd
still be dewy-eyed about doing the decent thing by her."

The elevator door opened, and Shayne said, "Somehow
I have a hunch we're going to learn a lot of interesting
things about Wanda Weatherby before this is over," as
they went through the lobby. "Most of it you won't be
able to print if my guess is right."

Outside, on the sidewalk, Rourke demanded, "Why did
you ask Ralph about Gurley? What's his connection with
Wanda?"

"Right now, I haven't any idea," Shayne admitted. "Except that he's damned anxious to keep her letter about
Ralph quiet."

"But—why? If Ralph doesn't even know him. And how
did Gurley find out about the letter?"

"All I can say is I don't know to both questions," Shayne
told him as they walked toward his car. When they reached
it Shayne lit a cigarette and gave him a brief résumé of
the anonymous telephone call and his later interview with
the gambler.

"How did you guess Gurley was behind this mug who
called you?" Rourke asked.

"Something I ran onto at Wanda's house before the police arrived. I won't tell you what it was, Tim, so that you can truthfully deny knowing anything about it if Will Gentry later accuses me of holding out on him. But I wish you would beat it down to headquarters and find out if Gentry picked up the same lead. Call me if you get anything hot."

"Sure, Mike," Rourke promised, and strolled back to his own car, adding over his shoulder, "If you don't hear from me sooner, I'll be at your office at nine o'clock."

"So will Gentry," said Shayne, "to pick up my mail for me."

Rourke spun around and took a couple of steps. "You're not going to give him Wanda's letter about Ralph?"

"I don't know what I'm going to do," Shayne growled. "You know as well as I do just how far I can push Will Gentry."

He left the reporter standing on the sidewalk, got in his car, gunned the motor, and hurried away to keep his midnight appointment.

CHAPTER SEVEN

THE TIME WAS a few minutes past twelve when Shayne strode into the lobby of his hotel-apartment house. The man on the desk beckoned to him as he headed toward the elevator. Shayne swung toward him with ragged brows lifted inquiringly.

"There's a lady waiting for you upstairs, sir. I sent her up a few minutes ago," he added apologetically. "But you always said I should use my own judgment."

"That's all right, Bennie," Shayne told him with a grin. "But I've never known you to unlock my room for a lady before."

Bennie licked his thin dry lips. "I don't recall any ladies wanting in to your room before, Mr. Shayne." The clerk grinned briefly, then added seriously, "This one is real class. She claimed she had an appointment."

"Green eyes?" asked Shayne negligently.

"What's that? N-No. But maybe they are, at that," he added after thinking for a moment. "Sort of grayish-green. And there was a phone call for you about half an hour ago. Some man—wouldn't leave his name, but wanted to know when you'd be in. I told him I didn't know, and he said he'd come over and wait. He seemed pretty anxious."

"Call me if he comes in," said Shayne. "And thanks, Bennie." He swung away and strode to the waiting elevator, got in, and went up to the second floor. He took his key out as he went down the corridor, put it back in his pocket when he saw his apartment door ajar and light streaming through the door. He pushed the door wide open when he reached it, and stood for a moment observing the woman sitting on the couch.

Her legs were crossed, and a short, expensive-looking fur jacket was thrown carelessly back from her shoulders. She wore a sheer black dress with a bright-orange scarf fluffed out at the throat, and was hatless. Her hair was long and straight, parted in the center and hanging down to her shoulders. It gleamed brightly in the overhead light, and the word "tawny" leaped into his mind. She had a high forehead and dark, thick brows and eyelashes. Her features were smooth and regular, her chin firm, her mouth wide and painted a deep shade of red that looked almost purple.

She appeared to be about thirty-five. Her head rested against the couch and her eyes were closed. She was smoking a cigarette, blowing smoke toward the ceiling, and was evidently unaware that she was being observed.

Shayne said, "Sorry to be late," pulling off his hat and tossing it on a wall hook near the door.

She opened her eyes and her lips formed a faint, questioning smile.

Shayne moved toward her, saying, "You were supposed to be a brunette. With limpid green eyes."

Her smile widened and the sensuous, sultry voice flowed out as it had over the telephone wire. "I hope you're not too disappointed, Michael Shayne."

"I hope I won't be. Drink?"

"Please." She leaned forward sinuously to crush out her cigarette in an ash tray beside the couch.

Shayne went past her to the liquor cabinet. "There's rye and cognac."

"Cognac, of course. Wouldn't it be a sacrilege to drink

anything else in Michael Shayne's apartment at midnight?" Her tone was light, but there was a nervous tremble that told the detective she was afraid in spite of her casual manner.

"Soda or water?" he asked.

"Straight, please. With some water on the side. And I need a big one before I lose my nerve and run out of here without telling you a word of what I came to say."

"We can't have that," said Shayne pleasantly. He took two four-ounce glasses from the shelf and filled one, handed it to her, adding, "I'll be right back with some ice water."

In the kitchen he put ice cubes in two tall glasses and filled them with water. When he turned, Sheila was standing in the doorway, watching him intently. Her glass was half-empty and spots of color flamed in her cheeks. Her eyes did look greenish, and wide and imploring.

"Are you the kind of man they say?" she asked breathlessly.

Shayne stopped in front of her with a glass in each hand. She didn't move from the threshold. He said, "I don't know, Sheila."

She looked up into his eyes, lips parted and chin lifted. "Why don't you kiss me? Don't you know that's what I want you to do? Hold me tight and comfort me and tell me I'm beautiful and promise to do what I'm going to ask you. Don't you know that's why I chose midnight? And came here to your place where we would be alone?" A pulse trembled in her rounded throat as she strained upward.

He said, "I didn't know, but I'm glad to have you tell me." He set the glasses aside on a kitchen table and put an arm around her. She went limp and buried her face against his chest and began to sob. The cognac glass fell from her hand and spilled liquor on the floor.

She was talking in a choked voice between sobs, but her words were not clear. He held her tightly for a moment, looking down somberly at the glistening, tawny hair against his chest. Then he sighed, picked her up in both arms, and carried her in to the couch. He put her down gently, and she huddled there with her hands over her face, sobbing convulsively.

Shayne returned for the glasses of water, retrieved her glass, and brought it back to the living-room where he refilled it and poured a drink for himself.

Sheila Martin sat erect after a while, dabbing at her eyes with a handkerchief. Shayne set her cognac and ice water on the low table in front of her and said, "Nothing is as bad as that, darling. Relax and make yourself kissable again if you're determined to seduce me."

She smiled wanly and blew her nose. "I've been holding it in so long," she said in a husky whisper. "I couldn't tell anyone, and it's been absolute hell. Then I got her letter tonight. You don't know Wanda Weatherby, do you?"

Shayne said, "No." He dropped into a chair close to the couch and stretched his legs out.

"When you do meet her you won't believe what I'm going to tell you," she burst out angrily. "She's vicious and depraved and evil. But you won't see that. No man ever does. She'll lie to you, and you'll believe her, even though you will already know the truth from me. I wish to God I had killed her," she went on violently, her face paling. "I should have done it right then when I threatened to. That's why she thinks it's I who tried to kill her, you see."

"I don't see much of anything," Shayne told her in a mild tone. "Why don't you start at the beginning?"

"I'll have to, I suppose. But first you'd better read this letter. You'll be getting a duplicate of it in the mail tomorrow morning, so you may as well read it now."

She reached for her handbag, opened it, and took out a square white envelope similar in size and shape to the one Ralph Flannagan had showed him. She handed it to him, saying, "It came by special messenger. Read it, and you'll understand why I'm so terribly upset."

Shayne took out the single sheet of folded paper and glanced at it, already suspecting what he would find. His hunch was right, for insofar as he could determine without comparing the two of them word for word, it was a duplicate of the carbon copy Flannagan had received, except her name and address was substituted for Flannagan's.

He frowned and pretended to read it carefully while he did some fast mental acrobatics. Was it possible that Jack Gurley had also received a duplicate by messenger, but with *his* name on it? That would explain a lot of things. If none of the three knew about the other letters—

He put speculation out of his mind as he refolded Sheila's letter and returned it to the envelope. Looking up to meet her eyes again, he said quietly, "If you haven't harmed her and don't plan to, why did this letter frighten you so?"

"Because you'll naturally want to see Wanda tomorrow as soon as you read the original of that, and she'll tell you —well, I don't know what she'll tell you about me. The truth, perhaps. Though I doubt it. If she can think up anything worse than the truth, she'll tell you *that*. And then you'll start checking up, and everything will come out, and Henry will be sure to find out. So you can see why I wish I had killed her," she ended defiantly.

Shayne leaned back and took a long drink of cognac. He indicated her glass and advised, "Take another sip and tell me why Wanda Weatherby suspects you want to murder her."

"She doesn't just suspect. She knows I do. I am going to tell you the truth, Mr. Shayne, even if I die of shame, because after you hear it maybe you'll be willing to disregard her letter in the morning and think of some way to prevent her from absolutely ruining my life."

Shayne said, "I never knew anyone to die of shame. How is she trying to ruin your life?"

"It goes back a long time. To nineteen thirty-five, in Detroit. I was eighteen and dewy-eyed from a farm in Iowa. My mother had just died, and I hated my stepfather, so I went away to the city to make my fortune." Her mouth twisted over the recollection. "Remember nineteen thirty-five, Mr. Shayne?"

He nodded. "I know what you mean."

"There weren't any jobs. Long lines of girls answering one advertisement. So, what does a girl do under those circumstances when her money runs out and she can't go back home?"

Shayne avoided her angry gaze. He frowned and suggested, "You tell me."

"It looks easy to a man. I've had lots of them say, 'My God, I wish I were a girl. You can bet *I* wouldn't go hungry.' But it isn't easy. Not when you're eighteen and fresh from the farm. You don't know how to start, damn it. You just don't know what to do. Not that girls don't think about it if they get hungry enough. That's when I met Wanda Weatherby. Just when I was down to my last penny and desperate enough to try anything.

"She was sitting beside me in a restaurant one day when

I had ordered a bowl of soup, the first thing I'd eaten in twenty-four hours, and I guess it showed. She was a few years older and beautiful and poised and, well, I guess I thought of her as being sophisticated. Anyway, she insisted on ordering me a lunch.

"Afterward, I went up to her apartment. I was ready for anything that afternoon. I wasn't so naïve that I thought she was just being generous. I'd heard about girls who like other girls, and I was all ready for even that. I didn't know what it was going to be, but I just didn't care."

Sheila Martin paused and took a big sip of cognac and a drink of ice water, then continued.

"Then when she sprung what she really wanted of me it didn't seem so bad after all. Because I was all keyed up for something worse, you see." Her voice trembled with earnestness, as though it was terribly important that she make him understand.

He said, "What did she want with you?"

"Well—for me to make moving pictures. She built it up gradually—all about how I didn't actually have to *do* anything. Just pose in the nude. And what did it matter? No one who knew me would ever see the picture. And she offered me a hundred dollars. A whole hundred dollars!" She caught her lower lip between her teeth, and tears glittered in her grayish eyes. She swallowed hard, then hurried on.

"Dear God! I can remember even now how magical that sounded. A hundred dollars just for a few afternoons' work. So I said yes, and she gave me ten dollars in advance. And two days later I did it. You know. One of those awful pornographic pictures they rent out for stag parties and smokers at men's clubs and conventions. Do you want to know exactly how awful it was?"

Shayne said moodily, "You don't have to go into details. Take another drink and relax. That was seventeen
years ago. I gather you didn't continue—make a career of
obscene movies."

"No. I invested the money in a shorthand and typing
course. I managed to get a job afterward, and everything
went all right. Wanda Weatherby and everything about
her gradually faded into the background like a bad dream
that actually hadn't happened. A year ago I met Henry
and we were married." She paused again and took another
sip from her glass.

"Then I met Wanda again," she continued, "here in
Miami, and quite by accident. She hardly seemed to have
changed at all. A little older, but you'd certainly never
guess she must be at least forty. Henry was with me. She
recognized me and began talking about old times in Detroit, just as though we'd been close friends. I had to in-
troduce him, and the next day she came out to our house."

She stopped talking and laced her fingers tightly. Spots
of color again flamed in her unrouged cheeks, and she
lowered her lids to cover the hatred in her eyes.

"And then?" Shayne prompted her.

"She wanted me to do it again," Sheila told him in a
listless voice. "I refused, of course, and begged her to leave
me alone, but she just laughed and said it was so hard to
find girls nowadays, with all the good jobs begging to be
taken.

"She was hard as nails. She just sat back and laughed
when I offered to pay her money to leave me alone. She
didn't want money. She wanted me. And when I flatly refused she threatened to show Henry the old film I made
in Detroit.

"It would kill Henry if he saw it. And I'll kill myself if

he ever does." Sheila Martin was leaning toward him, her body tense, and her face pale again. "That's when I went out of my mind and told Wanda I'd kill her if she ever did that. But it didn't frighten her at all. She just said it was up to me to decide. And I have until next week. She still has some of those old films, you see, and still rents them out. Next week there's going to be a special party at the Sportsman's Club where Henry works, and she'll either give them the one of *me*—or a different one. I have until next Friday to make up my mind," she ended, and sank back limply.

"Your husband works for Jack Gurley?" Shayne asked sharply.

"He's a waiter there. And when they have these special parties he has to work overtime to serve drinks, and he will have to see the pictures with the rest of them. You can see how viciously clever she is. She figured out that way of doing it without actually going to Henry and telling him. She doesn't have to appear in it at all. He'll just see the picture and that will be the end of everything. But I won't let her. I'll kill her first."

"Having failed twice already?" Shayne asked quietly.

"No. I haven't done anything. I don't know what she means in her letter. I've been crazy with worry, but I don't even know where she lives. All I have is a telephone number and I've called her three times to beg her not to do it. She won't even talk to me, just asks me if I'm ready to do what she wants, then hangs up when I try to plead with her.

"She's a devil, Mr. Shayne. She doesn't deserve to live. I don't think a jury would convict me if I killed her, not if they knew the truth. But that would be just as bad, because the whole story would come out and Henry would know, and nothing would be gained. So what am I going to do? What are you going to do about her letter?"

Shayne said, "I don't know yet. If you're telling me the truth—"

"I am," she cried huskily. "I swear I am. Do you think I *wanted* to tell anyone a thing like that? If I pay you a thousand dollars, can *I* be your client instead of her? Maybe you could get the film and destroy it—do something to keep her from letting Henry see it." She opened her purse and took out a handful of bills. "I haven't got all of it yet. But I can get the rest in a few days. If you'll take this much as down payment—"

Shayne waved it aside. "First, I want to know what you did tonight after telephoning me."

"I was out trying to raise this much money. There's six hundred and twenty dollars here. That's why I didn't want to see you until midnight. I knew what I had to do as soon as I hung up, and I called a friend who lives down the street and told her I had to raise a thousand dollars by midnight. She helped me—gave me all the cash she had— sixty dollars, then drove around with me to different friends of hers and mine borrowing whatever they could spare."

"How soon did you see your friend after phoning me?"

"Right away. Within five minutes. Henry is working, you see, and I went right over. It was just a few minutes when Betty and I started out."

"Will this Betty corroborate that?"

"Of course she will. Betty Hornsby is my best friend. Why? Does it matter?"

"It does," the detective told her. "Can you tell me the other friends you visited?"

"Certainly. I made a list of how much I got from each

one."

"I'll want the list, and your friend Betty's address. It matters a whole lot, Sheila," he said slowly, "because Wanda Weatherby was murdered tonight between ten and ten-thirty."

Sheila Martin was still leaning toward him with the money in her outstretched hand. She stared at him without moving for a long moment. Then she murmured, "Thank God," and slid forward on her knees, clutched at the arm of her chair, and pressed her forehead against it.

The telephone rang. Shayne jumped up and hurried to answer it.

The desk clerk's excited voice tumbled into Shayne's ears. "They're going up, Mr. Shayne. The chief of police and that reporter friend of yours. Just getting in the elevator. They didn't even stop at the desk."

Shayne barked, "Thanks," and slammed the receiver down. He leaped to Sheila's side, dragged her erect, and said swiftly, "Kiss me good—and ruffle your hair. Hurry. Finish your drink and spill a few drops down the front of your dress. The cops are on their way up here, and if we're going to keep you out of this we've got to make them think they're interrupting a necking-party."

"Oh, God," she breathed, and was instantly alert. She stood on tiptoe, flung her arms around his neck, and put her parted lips hard against his. Shayne kissed her back, all the while tousling her tawny hair. Her eyes were shining when she drew back and she said, "I liked that, Michael. If you can get rid of them—"

"I liked it, too." He grinned and gave her a shove toward the couch, saying, "Drink up—and make like a loose woman."

She said tremulously, "It won't be hard, Michael Shayne.

You make me feel like one."

Shayne grabbed up his own drink and finished it off, snatched a bottle from the cabinet and set it on the table in front of the couch. He shrugged out of his jacket and tossed it on a chair, jerked open the neckband of his shirt and pulled his tie awry as heavy footsteps sounded in the corridor outside.

He looked at Sheila and nodded approvingly. She lolled back on the couch with her skirt well above one knee, and her long hair slid forward over one side of her face. Her lipstick was smeared, and the picture was complete.

Shayne was refilling his glass with cognac when an authoritative knock sounded on the door.

CHAPTER EIGHT

SHAYNE DROPPED onto the couch beside Sheila with glass in hand. He slid one arm around her shoulders and pinched her cheek, and waited for Gentry's knock to be repeated, muttering in her ear, "Play it up the best you can, darling. We're both tight and plenty sore at being interrupted."

Sheila didn't reply, but pressed his hand hard against her cheek. She was warm and she smelled good, and Shayne wondered how much she loved her husband.

Will Gentry knocked again, and more insistently, and the deep rumble of his voice penetrated the door. "Open up, Mike. It's Will Gentry."

Shayne drank half his cognac, gave Sheila a final pat, and said angrily, "It's the chief of police, honey. I'll have to open up. You sit tight."

He got up and started toward the door as Gentry pounded on it again. Shayne growled, "All right! Damn it. You don't have to break the door down." He turned the knob and opened the door about six inches, holding it firmly against Gentry's thrust and peering out with an angry scowl.

"What in hell's the matter, Will? You might let a man know—"

Gentry said, "Want to ask you a couple of questions." His gaze went from the glass in the detective's hand to his disheveled appearance and the smear of lipstick on his mouth. "Sorry if I interrupted anything important," he added gruffly, "but you do choose the damnedest time for your tomcatting. Send your floosie in the bedroom if you're ashamed for Tim and me to see her. If she isn't already there," he ended.

Shayne drew himself up, pretending outraged dignity, hiccuped, and said, "She's no floosie, and this isn't what you think at all. It's just your foul mind." He threw the door open grandly as Gentry plodded through, and the redhead gave Timothy Rourke a broad wink, and continued, "Certainly don't want you to think I'm ashamed of introducing my friends." He closed the door and said, "Sylvia, meet Chief Will Gentry, and Mr. Rourke from the *Daily News*."

She was lolling against the couch with a cigarette dangling from her mouth. Tossing her head, she giggled, "Glad to make your acquaintance, I'm sure."

Gentry nodded curtly and asked Shayne, "Can't she go in the other room for a few minutes? This is important."

Rourke had acknowledged the introduction with "Hi, Sylvia," and stood to one side, appraising Sheila Martin with saturnine approval.

Shayne tossed off the rest of his cognac and waved a big hand vaguely. "Make yourselves right at home. Fix Will a drink, Tim—and help yourself." He went to the couch, wavering a trifle but holding himself erect, leaned over Sheila, and said tenderly, " 'Scuse us for a minute, sweet. Gotta talk business with the cops."

He caught her hands and helped her up, went with her to the bedroom and steered her inside, half-closed the door as he switched on the light. She turned and pressed herself against him, pulling his face down, saying, "Let's make it look good."

Shayne held her tightly and again she kissed him with

parted, moving lips. They were both trembling when he released her and stepped back. He considered her gravely for a second, then nodded and went out without speaking, pulling the door shut behind him.

Will Gentry was seated solidly on the couch with his hands resting on his knees. "Are you sober enough to answer a couple of questions, Mike?"

"Perfectly sober. Ask your questions, for God's sake, and then beat it."

"Sure, sure," said Gentry soothingly. "If you'd told Tim or me you had a date, I wouldn't have bothered you this way."

"I wasn't aware," Shayne snapped, "that I was supposed to clear my dates through official channels." He lurched as he reached for his glass, recovered himself, and filled it with exceeding care.

Rourke came in from the kitchen with two long, cold drinks, and handed one to Gentry. "It was Will's idea to bust in on you like this, but you shouldn't be so damned cagey, Mike. Hell, I thought you were spending all your extra time with Lucy these nights."

"Lucy is a nice girl," said Shayne seriously. "And so is Sylvia a nice girl. Here's to nice girls." He lifted his glass high, waited until the others took a drink, took a couple of swallows from his glass, and sank into a chair. "What are your questions, Will?"

"You told me tonight you'd never met Wanda Weatherby. Didn't know anything at all about her except the one phone call asking you to see her. Is that right?"

"Something like that," Shayne told him placidly, "because it happened to be the truth."

"Then why did she pay you a thousand bucks yesterday?"

"Did she?"

"You know damned well she did."

"I know nothing of the sort," Shayne contradicted him flatly.

"The final stub in her checkbook, dated yesterday, shows a check made out to Michael Shayne for one grand—and a notation saying 'Retainer.' "

Shayne shrugged and reminded the chief, "Lucy told you that Wanda tried to call me twice during the afternoon, and then said she was writing me a letter. Even a dumb cop should be able to deduce that just possibly she enclosed a retainer with the letter."

Gentry's face turned an angry red. "All right, damn it, that may be the answer. But here's another question. What took you straight to the Sportsman's Club from her place to ask Jack Gurley about her? How did you know about her connection with Gurley?"

"*Is* there a connection?" Shayne stopped pretending to be drunk. He was sure the by-play with Sheila had gone over and that neither of the men suspected she was anything more than a drinking companion.

"You must have thought so when you went there."

"Maybe I wanted a free drink, or felt like tossing away a few bucks on Gurley's crooked wheels."

"Cut it out, Mike," roared Gentry. "I know you jumped him about Wanda."

"Did he tell you so?"

"As good as. The moment I braced him he got sore and growled, 'So that damned shamus shot off his big mouth, eh?' "

"There are other detectives in Miami," Shayne countered. "And my mouth isn't so big as to make that a positive identification."

Gentry's agate eyes were cold. "Give me a straight answer to a straight question," he demanded, "if you want to get back in the bedroom tonight. What sent you to Gurley?"

"I'll trade," Shayne offered cheerfully. "Tell me what tipped you off and I'll tell you mine."

Will Gentry hesitated, knowing the redhead's stubbornness from long experience, and his disinclination to give information under pressure. Right now, the dead woman's attempt to see Shayne before she died and her letter to him, now in the mail, were the only angles he had to work on. He said cautiously, "If I go that far will you promise not to make any trouble about me reading your mail in the morning?"

Shayne considered for a moment, conscious that the reporter was listening and awaiting his reply, conscious of the check in his pocket—the retainer he had accepted from Ralph Flannagan on condition that his name be kept out of the murder investigation. He sighed and said reluctantly, "After I read it first."

"With me watching you open it to see I get it all?" pressed Gentry.

"Sure. You know I wouldn't hold out anything important, Will." He glanced at Rourke, keeping his face blandly impervious to the angry disgust the reporter showed.

"That's a direct promise," said Gentry heavily, "and I'll hold you to it. Okay. Among the papers in Wanda Weatherby's desk we found a series of newspaper stories from a clipping bureau that were all about Gurley and his family. That's why *I* went to him."

"How did he explain them?"

"I didn't tell him— Wait a minute," the chief expostulated. "This was a horse trade."

"You didn't tell him about the clippings?" Shayne said angrily. "You went away from there with him believing I was the one who sent you? Damn it, Will, you really put the finger on me that time. Of all the lousy tricks to play on a guy who's supposed to be your friend!"

"I didn't put the finger on you," roared Gentry, his face purpling with anger. "Gurley jumped to that conclusion himself."

"And you left him believing it. Don't forget that if I wake up dead from lead poisoning tomorrow."

"You fingered yourself by going to him first," Gentry flared. "Don't forget *that*. If you'd keep your nose out of my homicide cases you wouldn't be asking for trouble."

"Maybe it's kind of my case, too, Will. She did call me for protection instead of going to the police when she was in fear of her life. Why? Answer me that." He leaned forward and pointed an accusing finger at the chief. "Because your lousy homicide department has such a stinking reputation, that's why. You ought to be damned glad there's someone a tax-paying citizen can turn to for help when they need it instead of giving me hell for solving your cases for you."

Chief Will Gentry took a drink of rye and water, and choked over it. He lowered his glass, sputtering with rage.

Timothy Rourke leaped into the breach with conciliatory words. "Shut up, both of you. Before you say any more that you don't mean. You're drunk, Mike."

"Like hell he's drunk," shouted Gentry. "He's just trying to get me sore enough to forget what I came here for. I'm waiting for that trade, shamus."

Shayne hesitated, his gray eyes bleak, the trenches deepening in his gaunt cheeks. He said, "It's been a long time since a friend of mine called me shamus."

Gentry said stubbornly, "I'm still waiting."

Shayne sighed. "Okay, Will. So we forget the friendship. I got the same tip you did. That Wanda Weatherby was collecting clippings on Gurley. And like you, I wondered why."

"How did you know about the clips?" Gentry demanded.

"I discovered her body and called in," Shayne reminded him evenly. "It was a few minutes before anybody got there. Do you think I sat down and twiddled my thumbs while I waited?"

"Hell, no. I'm sure you went through everything you could find and carried away anything you thought might help you solve the case and prevent us from doing it."

"I left the clips for you," said Shayne dryly.

"How did Gurley explain them to you?"

"He didn't."

"What did he say about them?"

"Why, just like you, Will, I didn't think it was good business to spring them on him right then."

"How else did you explain your interest in the Weatherby woman—your reason for going to him?"

"That wasn't included in the trade," said Shayne calmly. "But I assure you I didn't put anyone else on the spot by intimating that he had sent me around."

Gentry opened his mouth to reply, but checked himself with an effort. He set his half-emptied highball glass down and heaved his bulky body up from the couch, asking gruffly, "You coming along, Tim?"

"I think maybe I'll stick around a few minutes," Rourke answered slowly, avoiding Shayne's eyes. "I'll finish this drink and find out if his blonde has a friend."

Gentry snorted and started for the door. The telephone rang, and the police chief stopped and turned back to listen while Shayne answered.

A girl's excited voice came over the wire. "Is this Michael Shayne? The detective?"

"Yeah."

"You don't know me, Mr. Shayne, but I'm Mary Devon. Helen Taylor's roommate."

"Yeh?" he repeated when she paused. He glanced sardonically at the reporter and police chief who were listening intently.

"Something terrible has happened," the girl's voice resumed and grew panicky as she hurried on. "Helen—I'm afraid she's dying, Mr. Shayne. I've called a doctor, but she keeps mumbling your name over and over. And something about Wanda Weatherby. I can't understand it at all, but maybe you'll know. You'd better hurry over here because I'm afraid—oh—that must be the doctor now."

"Where are you?" Shayne demanded.

She named a small hotel on Miami Avenue, gave him the room number, and Shayne said, "Right away."

He slammed the receiver down and leaped to his feet muttering angrily, "This is a hell of a mess. Sylvia's husband. He's on his way here now. You two guys can stay if you want, but I'm getting out of here fast."

CHAPTER NINE

MICHAEL SHAYNE STRAIGHTENED his tie, grabbed his jacket, and shrugged into it on his way to the bedroom. He jerked the door open and said to Sheila, "We've got to get out of here in a hurry, babe," in a loud, excited voice. "Your husband's on his way here with blood in his eye."

She was lying on the bed, fully clothed. "Wh-at?" She sat up slowly, her eyes round and staring in disbelief.

Shayne knew the two men were listening with amusement, and he made his voice angry. "Come on, for God's sake! Pete just phoned to tip me off." He caught her by the arm and rushed her out, stopping to snatch up her fur jacket from the couch.

Gentry and Rourke were at the door. Rourke grinned evilly and suggested, "Want me to smuggle her out, Mike? You can wipe that lipstick off your face and try to convince the guy you've been spending the evening with a good book."

"Thanks," Shayne snapped. "I'd rather be out when he gets here." He pushed past the two men, dragged Sheila along with him to the elevator, jabbed impatiently at the elevator button, saying harshly, "Damn it, you told me he was all tied up for the night."

Having no idea what the detective was talking about or why he was making this pretense, Sheila played up to him by looking as frightened and disconcerted as possible. She said, plaintively, "I don't know how on earth he knew I was here, darling. I just don't understand it, but please let's hurry."

The elevator came and the quartet got in and stood in awkward silence as it went down. Shayne got out first and strode swiftly across the lobby with his arm linked firmly in Sheila's, calling over his shoulder, "See you at the office in the morning, Will."

His car was parked at the front entrance. He pushed Sheila in the front seat, trotted around, and got in and sped away before Chief Gentry and Rourke emerged from the doorway.

"Had to do it that way," he explained before she could start asking questions. "That call was from a dying woman —something about Wanda Weatherby, and I had to get out fast and shake Will Gentry at the same time. Only thing I could think of was the outraged-husband gag."

Sheila sighed with relief. "You did it very efficiently," she told him. "As though you've had practice. And neither of them seemed surprised."

"Sorry to have to characterize you as an adulterous female," Shayne muttered, swinging north onto First Avenue.

"Don't be." Her voice was light—almost gay. "For a little while back there I'm not sure I would have minded dreadfully being one."

"There's Henry," Shayne reminded her, his tone as light as hers.

"I know. And I do love him. I guess I'm awful. I guess all women are—at times."

"Not awful. Just honest enough to admit sometimes that monogamy isn't all it's cracked up to be. A very interesting topic of discussion. But right now I'm chasing down a murderer and I suggest you hop out here at Flagler." He slowed for the main street of the city, and Sheila agreed in a subdued voice.

"I guess I'd better. But you didn't take my money for a retainer."

"Forget the money right now." Shayne reached past her to open the door as he braked the car. "After I check your alibi will be time enough for that. I've got a green light," he pointed out.

Sheila Martin bit her underlip and slid out. She started to say something, but Shayne gunned the motor to slide across Flagler as the light turned yellow. He drove north eight blocks, then swung left to one-way Miami Avenue and back half a block to pull up in front of the shabby Metro Hotel.

He entered a smelly, empty lobby. The desk was deserted, but a printed sign propped upon it read: *Ring Bell for Clerk.* Shayne strode to the stairs, went up two flights and down a narrow corridor searching for the number Mary Devon had given him over the phone.

Number 32 was next to the rear and the door stood ajar with light streaming through. Shayne tapped and pushed it open upon a small bedroom.

A girl reclined on the bed, crying quietly. A man stood beside her with a doctor's bag in his hand. He wore bedroom slippers and a gray bathrobe over seersucker pajamas, and Shayne realized that the call had, indeed, been urgent.

The slim, balding doctor blinked nearsightedly at the detective and said to the girl in a weary, nasal voice, "I will have to report this to the police, of course. Leave everything just as it is until they arrive."

Shayne stood blocking the doorway. He said, "Miss Devon?"

The girl gazed at him through her tears and nodded

listlessly. "Are you Mr. Shayne? Helen is— The doctor says—"

"Michael Shayne?" The doctor lifted his brows expressively and looked relieved. "As you see, I came as quickly as I could, but it was too late. The young lady was—ah—D.O.A. You understand the importance of leaving everything untouched for the police. I'm Doctor Brinstead. The body is in the adjoining room."

Shayne acknowledged the introduction, then asked, "Poison?"

"Indubitably. Definitely an alkaloid, and almost certainly strychnine." He turned to the weeping girl. "You mustn't blame yourself, Miss Devon. I'm afraid nothing could have saved your friend at the time you discovered her condition. I'll make a full report to the police."

"Suicide?" Shayne demanded, still blocking the doorway as the doctor made a tentative move to leave.

"Probably. Most deaths by strychnine poisoning are. It's possible it was taken accidentally, though Miss Devon insists there were no medicines at hand containing the poison."

"Could it be murder?"

"That's a matter for the police to determine, Mr. Shayne. It would be my guess that at least half a grain was ingested sometime between one and four hours prior to death. Analysis of the stomach contents is very important, and this should be reported at once."

Shayne nodded and stood aside to let the doctor pass. He crossed over and sat down beside the girl and said quietly, "Please tell me everything you can before the police get here. We won't have any chance to talk after that. First, what exactly did your friend say about me and about Wanda Weatherby?"

"Nothing, really. That is, nothing I could understand. Oh, it's so horrible, Mr. Shayne!" she wailed. "I just can't realize Helen is dead. She was delirious and sort of incoherent when I came home about twelve—and having convulsions. Oh! It was awful! And in between convulsions she would moan your name—and that woman's. Wanda Weatherby. I never heard of her before, but I did know you were a famous detective. So I called Doctor Brinstead first, and then telephoned you to come. I guess she was actually dying when I was talking to you."

"Who was Helen Taylor?" Shayne asked. "And who are you? Tell me about yourselves—and make it as fast as you can. You see," he added bitterly, "Wanda Weatherby was also murdered tonight—before I could reach her."

His last words struck through Mary Devon's grief. She lifted her head and looked at him, her eyes terrified. "Then you really think Helen was—was—"

"Murdered," Shayne supplied for her. "Unless she killed Wanda and then committed suicide. Perhaps that's what she wanted to tell me. Try to remember every word she said so we can judge whether that could be it."

"I just don't know," Mary said helplessly. "But Helen wouldn't *murder* anybody. Not ever. She was sweet and nice—and so full of fun—" Her voice choked up, and Shayne got out a handkerchief and pressed it into her hand.

"Blow your nose and get hold of yourself," he urged. He got up and restlessly crossed the bedroom to an open door at the rear leading into the bathroom. The connecting door was closed. He opened it onto a duplicate of the other.

A figure lay on the bed with a coverlet drawn over it. There was some disorder here, with clothes and towels strewn about on chairs, and Shayne's face was masklike as he went around to the side of the bed and drew back the spread.

Helen Taylor was young, and had probably been an extremely attractive girl. Now, her body was arched rigidly in a final convulsion and her features were horribly contracted, the skin a characteristic dark blue shading to gray on the throat and breast.

He replaced the coverlet and returned somberly to the other room. Mary was sitting erect, wiping her eyes, and she managed a smile when the redhead re-entered her room.

"I just don't know what to tell you," she burst out. "I saw Helen about seven-thirty when I had to go out, and she seemed exceptionally cheerful. We've been roommates here for almost six months, and the best of friends. I had no premonition of anything like this. I knew she was going out later, but when I left she said she'd probably be home before I came in. When I did come back, she was—"

"Do you know where she went?" Shayne interrupted.

"No." Mary hesitated a trifle. "It was something that came up unexpectedly—just before I went out, I think. She had a telephone call while I was dressing, and before that she had planned to spend the evening at home. The call made her happy, and I had the impression that it was—well, a man. But she didn't tell me anything except that she would be going out, and I didn't question her."

"Any particular man?"

"No—not that I know of. Helen was popular and had lots of dates, but I didn't know about anything serious. You see, we've been in radio quite a while, and we meet lots of people at the stations and on different programs."

"In radio?" Shayne pounced on that small crumb of

information. "Actresses?"

"Yes. That's how we met. And it made it pleasant to share these two bedrooms."

"Do you know Ralph Flannagan?"

"Oh, yes." Mary looked at him in surprise. "He produces the show I'm on regularly. 'Fragments From Life.' It's just a daytime serial, but really quite well written and produced."

"Did Miss Taylor work on his show?"

"No. That is, not one of the regular roles. She did do bit parts on it now and then."

"So she knew Flannagan?"

"Yes."

"How well? Did she ever date him?"

"Ralph? I don't think so. He never—that is, I never heard of him showing any interest in any of the girls on his show. I *think* he's engaged to marry his sponsor's daughter. That's what they say. Some of them think that —well, that's the reason he's got a sponsor. But it is a good program with a high rating, and most of that talk is just jealousy."

"Do either of you do any television work?" Shayne asked abruptly.

"We haven't yet. There actually isn't much television here. Some film companies come down on location, but no live shows."

"Do you know if Flannagan did any television?"

"I don't think so. Everybody in radio is interested in it, of course, and wants to get a foothold, but there isn't much opportunity here yet."

"Have you heard any rumors of anyone going in for making pornographic kinescopes for private showing? Anyone being approached for that sort of thing?"

"No." Mary Devon wrinkled her brow and appeared to be answering honestly. "I certainly haven't been. And Helen never mentioned anything like that."

"And you have absolutely no idea where she was between the time you went out at seven-thirty and your return about midnight?"

"No, I haven't, Mr. Shane."

"Did she receive a letter by special messenger this evening?"

"Not while I was here. And I had the impression she was leaving right after I did."

"Try once more," Shayne urged her, "to remember if you haven't ever heard the name of Wanda Weatherby before."

Mary shook her head slowly. "I've been racking my brains ever since Helen started mumbling her name. But I just don't know."

"The police will be here in a very few minutes," Shayne warned her. "Tell them the truth—just as you've told me. Don't try to hide anything. And if you remember anything important—or learn anything at all, please telephone me."

He started for the door. She stopped him to ask in a troubled voice, "Shall I tell them you were here?"

"You'll have to. The doctor will, and it's all right. You had every reason to telephone me. I'll be in touch." He waved a big hand reassuringly and hurried out, down the stairs, and into the empty lobby. A police car pulled in to the curb behind him as he got into his car and hurried away.

CHAPTER TEN

MICHAEL SHAYNE PARKED on a quiet side street just east of the Boulevard in front of his secretary's apartment building. Glancing up at the second-floor windows as he got out he saw that they were dark.

In the small foyer he pressed her button three long rings and waited with his hand on the doorknob. He turned it when her buzzer released the latch, went in and up the stairs two at a time and down the hall where Lucy Hamilton waited for him in the doorway.

She wore a quilted robe over flowered pajamas, and her brown hair was brushed back neatly from her face and caught with a ribbon in the back. Barefooted and with no make-up, she looked absurdly childlike as she stepped back inside exclaiming, "I'd just got back to sleep, Michael. What's been happening?"

"I'll bring you up to date in a minute." He ruffled her hair and dropped a light kiss on her lips. "But here's something first," he added, striding to the telephone stand. He lifted the directory and began leafing through it in search of Ralph Flannagan's number. He found it listed, a direct line that did not go through the building switchboard.

Lucy stood beside him, her eyes bright with curiosity. "What on earth?"

"Here—take the receiver and dial this number. I'll call it off for you. And start talking fast when a man answers," he directed. "Say, 'This is Helen Taylor and I've just heard over the radio about Wanda Weatherby and I have to see you at once.' That's all. Make your voice sound excited and worried. Don't answer any questions except to insist you're Helen Taylor and must see him. Got it?"

"Let's see— I'm Helen Taylor and I've just heard about Wanda Weatherby over the radio and have to see him at once. Who, Michael?"

"His name is Ralph Flannagan, but I don't know whether Helen would call him Ralph or Mr. Flannagan or darling, so try to skip it." He called the numbers as she dialed, then stepped aside to light a cigarette.

Lucy waited a moment, then spoke rapidly and excitedly into the mouthpiece. He watched her face tensely when she finished, heard the faint crackle of Flannagan's voice over the wire.

"I *am* Helen," she insisted after a moment. "And I must talk to you at once." She listened again for a moment, then hung up. "My voice must have sounded all wrong," she said ruefully. "He simply didn't believe I was Helen Taylor, and acted as though he didn't know what any of it was about. He said he would call me back to check, and then hung up. He sounded frightened and angry, Michael. Does that help?"

"It might." Shayne stood for a moment rubbing his angular jaw, his gaze remote and withdrawn. At this moment, only one person other than the police, Dr. Brinstead, the girl's roommate, and himself could possibly know that Helen was dead—or had reason to suspect she was so ill from poison that it was unlikely she could be using the phone.

Shayne said slowly, "Try exactly the same thing on Jack Gurley at the Sportsman's Club, Lucy. You'll know better what to listen for when I tell you that Helen Taylor died about twenty minutes ago from strychnine. If she was murdered, the person who fed her the poison is the only one who knows about it."

Lucy nodded uncertainly. "Your Mr. Flannagan seemed awfully certain I wasn't Helen Taylor. On the other hand, he was going to call her back. Would he do that if he knew she was already dead?"

"He might. If his nerves were steady enough and he thought fast enough. On the other hand, it's what an innocent man would normally do if your voice didn't sound right. Try it on Gurley, anyway. Those are the only two strings I've got right now. Shall I mix you a drink?"

"A small one. Isn't Jack Gurley the man they call The Lantern?"

"Yeh."

Shayne went into the kitchen and took a bottle of cognac from a high shelf where he knew it would be. He poured a large straight drink for himself, put a smaller portion into a glass with a cube of ice and a little water, carried them back into the living-room in time to hear Lucy say, "No. This is a personal call. Just tell him it's Helen Taylor."

She glanced aside with lifted brows as Shayne made himself comfortable on the couch, with the two glasses on the coffee table. Then she said over the telephone, "This is Helen Taylor and I've just heard over the radio about Wanda Weatherby and I have to see you at once."

She listened while Shayne moodily smoked a cigarette and visualized the gambler at the other end of the wire. Then she protested, "I can't tell you any more over the phone. But this is Helen Taylor and I must see you at once." After listening again and for a longer period, she said, "Very well, then," and hung up.

A frown puckered her forehead as she crossed to the

couch. "I guess that was a blank, Michael, though you can't really tell about a man like that. He said he didn't know me and why did I think he was interested in talking about Wanda Weatherby. When I wouldn't tell him, he said why didn't I write him a letter, and hung up." Lucy sat down beside him and curled her bare feet up under her robe and reached for the glass of watered cognac.

She said, "Now start at the beginning and tell me everything. Who is Wanda Weatherby—and what does Helen Taylor have to do with anything?"

"First, you tell me about those phone calls this afternoon. Did Wanda give you any idea why she wanted to see me?"

"No. Except it was important that she see you at once."

"Did you suggest her calling me at home later?"

"No. When she called the second time she said she was writing you a letter which you'd receive in the morning. From that, I supposed it could wait overnight."

Shayne nodded and took a long drink of cognac. "Something came up," he told Lucy moodily, "to make her realize it couldn't wait overnight. She called me at home at ten o'clock—after I had already received two calls from other people who knew about the letter she had written me." He settled back and related the events from the time he entered his apartment that evening to find the telephone ringing.

Lucy listened attentively, and when he finished, she said, "I turned on my radio after Chief Gentry woke me to ask about you. There was a flash about Wanda Weatherby on the eleven-thirty newscast. From what Mr. Flannagan and that Sheila person told you about her, it sounds as though she was asking for just what she got. If Sheila is as nice as you say," she added thoughtfully, "it would be horrible to drag up something like that one indiscretion out of her past—now that she's happily married."

"I don't know how nice Sheila is," Shayne told her irritably. "And I don't go too far on the happy-marriage angle. The way she cuddled up to me—"

"But she was frightened to death by Wanda's letter, and desperately needed your help," Lucy interrupted. "Besides, you're not so hard to cuddle up to, Michael," she added, her brown eyes crinkling with laughter.

"U-m-m," Shayne muttered absently. He got up and went to the phone, saying, "I forgot about the man who said he was coming to my hotel to see me. I'd better check."

He dialed the number and said, "Mike Shayne," when the clerk answered.

The clerk said rapidly, "There's a man waiting here in the lobby, Mr. Shayne—and there was a call for you just a minute ago. Mr. Ralph Flannagan wants you to call him at once. It's very important."

"Who's the man waiting?"

"He didn't give his name," said the clerk. "He's been waiting about half an hour. Said he was the one who had phoned while you were out."

Shayne said, "Put him on now."

After a short wait a richly unctuous voice came over the wire. "Mr. Shayne? How soon may I see you? It's very important."

"Who's speaking?" Shayne interrupted.

"I—ah— Please keep this completely confidential, Mr. Shayne. This is Donald J. Henderson speaking. I must have your advice on a matter of the gravest importance immediately."

"What sort of a matter? I'm tangled up with a case and don't know when I'll be in."

"It concerns—ah—a letter you will receive in the morning post."

"From Wanda Weatherby?" Shayne demanded.

"How did you— Then you've been in touch with her?" Henderson's tone took on a note of aggrieved asperity. "I have no idea what she may have told you, but I assure you there is not a word of truth in it. Why, I don't even know the woman, Mr. Shayne. This is the most preposterous—"

"Hold it until I get there," Shayne snapped. "Within half an hour, I hope."

He hung up and growled, "Another one, Lucy. One of our most esteemed civic leaders this time. Donald Henderson. My God! The woman must have sent out her letters wholesale. Henderson claims he doesn't even know her." He paused, his hand on the receiver, started to ask his secretary the number she had dialed for Ralph Flannagan, then remembered the digits he had called to her. He lifted the instrument and dialed.

The radio producer sounded much relieved to hear his voice. "Mr. Shayne! The most extraordinary thing has happened. I thought you should know at once. I've been trying to get you."

"What is it?" he asked, grinning at Lucy.

"A short time ago I had a telephone call from some woman who claimed she was Helen Taylor and who insisted she wanted to talk to me about Wanda. I do know a girl named Helen Taylor—in a business way. She's an actress who has done bit parts on my show occasionally, and I'm certain it wasn't her voice. She refused to say anything more except that she wanted to talk to me about Wanda. I hung up and checked by calling Miss Taylor's number.

"A man answered the phone, Mr. Shayne." Flannagan's

voice trembled with excitement and fear. "He sounded—well—gruff and official. Maybe it was my imagination, but I thought it was a policeman. He demanded to know who I was when I asked for Miss Taylor, and kept on asking questions when I wouldn't tell him, and I had a feeling he was trying to keep me on the line while the call was traced. So I hung up.

"What do you suppose has happened? What connection can there be between Miss Taylor and Wanda? And who could the woman be who called me?"

"How positive are you that it wasn't Miss Taylor?" Shayne asked casually.

"Voices are my business, Mr. Shayne. I suppose one can't be absolutely positive over the telephone, but there's the added fact that Miss Taylor was here for an audition this evening, and I listened to her very carefully, evaluating the quality, the timbre and nuances—"

"Wait a minute," said Shayne sharply. "You say she was at your place this evening?"

"Yes. She and two other actresses. I told you—"

"What time?" Shayne interrupted. "It may be very important."

"Why—about eight, I think."

"After the letter from Wanda arrived by messenger? Are you quite sure you didn't mention it to her, Flannagan?"

"Positive. I don't discuss personal affairs with girls who come for auditions," he said stiffly.

"Is it possible she could have seen the letter without your knowledge?"

"Why I—think it extremely unlikely. It may possibly have been lying about while she was here, but she didn't impress me as the sort of girl who would surreptitiously read my personal mail."

"What time did she leave your place?"

"About eight-twenty, I should say."

"Alone?"

"Yes. See here, Mr. Shayne, what do you think—"

"What sort of mood was she in?" the detective cut in sharply.

"Excellent," Flannagan assured him. "You see, the audition went well, and I practically assured her she would get the part."

"You'll have to report this to the police," Shayne told him, "as soon as you read about her death in the morning paper."

"Helen—Taylor's—death?" The radio producer's voice was inexpressibly shocked. "Good Lord! What possible connection could there have been between her and Wanda? And who could have phoned me?"

"My secretary," said Shayne grimly, "and you can leave that fact out of the story when you talk to the police. That is, if you still hope to avoid being involved in Wanda Weatherby's murder."

"Certainly, Mr. Shayne. And you do think we can avoid it, don't you?"

"I'm going to do my best," Shayne told him wearily. "I have to get started right now. You'd better get some sleep." He hung up abruptly and went back to the couch, his thumb and forefinger tugging at his left earlobe.

"What do you think now, Michael?" Lucy asked eagerly.

"It's all just a little bit more tangled than before," he answered absently. "Helen Taylor was at Flannagan's apartment between eight and eight-twenty. At midnight she dies in convulsions, moaning something about me and Wanda Weatherby. If Gentry sees that letter in the morning, he really will tear into Flannagan."

"But you'll have to let him see it, Michael," Lucy insisted. "You told me you promised him you would."

Shayne picked up his drink, took a long sip, set it down, and leaned his head back on the couch. He closed his eyes and thought for a long moment, then jerked himself erect and gave Lucy a crooked smile.

"Look—what I promised Will, in his own words, was that I would not make any trouble about his reading my mail in the morning. Get out your portable," he went on cheerfully, "and some feminine notepaper—the kind that folds. Preferably white, with square envelopes, if you have it."

"I received three boxes for Christmas presents," she told him. "One of them was white, if I remember correctly. But what on earth—"

"Be ready when I get back, angel," he said. He came swiftly to his feet, tossed off his drink, and taking his glass with him strode into the kitchenette for a refill.

When he returned, Lucy Hamilton had the portable on her lap and a sheet of white notepaper rolled in. She held a square envelope up and asked, "Will this do?"

"Fine." He sat down beside her and began dictating:

"Dear Mr. Shayne: I enclose one thousand dollars and the original of another letter to you which will be self-explanatory. The thousand is for your retainer in case something happens to me before I am able to talk to you. Very truly yours, Wanda Weatherby."

Lucy shook her head worriedly, but her eyes sparkled when she finished typing and looked at him. "Is that all, Michael? I don't understand why Chief Gentry could find anything in a note like—"

"Wait a minute," Shayne said, a wry smile spreading

his wide mouth. "Add a postscript."

Lucy rolled the paper down, wrote, *P.S.*, and he dictated:

"I wish to retain you because I have absolutely no faith in the Miami police department which has a reputation for being the most corrupt and inefficient in the United States."

Lucy Hamilton gasped, stopped short of finishing the sentence, and exclaimed, "Michael Shayne! If you're planning to do with this letter what I *think* you are, Will Gentry will have kittens all over the office when he reads it."

"Finish it," Shayne told her blandly. "Will deserves just that—for suspecting me of holding out on him."

Lucy finished typing the postscript, rolled the sheet from the portable, laid it on the table, and started to pick up an envelope.

"Hold it," Shayne ordered. "Put in another sheet of paper," and when she complied, he closed his eyes and tried to recall the exact wording of the two letters Ralph Flannagan and Sheila Martin had showed him. He dictated slowly:

"Dear Mr. Shayne: I tried to call you at your office two different times today, but you were out and it is five o'clock now so I am going to write you instead. I enclose one thousand dollars as a retainer for you in case anything happens to me tonight, and that will be your fee for convicting Jack Gurley at the Sportsman's Club of my murder, because he will be the guilty one. He has tried to murder me twice already, and I am desperately afraid he will try again tonight.

I am going to send him a carbon of this letter by special messenger so he'll know I've told you about it, and maybe he will decide not to when he realizes you will suspect him.

I will telephone you first thing in the morning for an appointment if I am still alive. Very truly yours, Wanda Weatherby."

Lucy asked, "Any postscript?" when she finished typing. Shayne shook his head, and she rolled the sheet from the portable.

"Now address an envelope to me at the office. Put her address in the usual place, but make a couple of mistakes in it and in my address. Ex out the errors so you'll be able to recognize this envelope from the one she mailed when they both arrive at the office tomorrow morning."

Lucy put the envelope in the portable and followed instructions. When she rolled it out and handed it to him, she said, "This really throws Mr. Gurley at Chief Gentry, Michael. And you don't even know that she wrote a letter like this about him."

"It's a fair assumption, angel. The two recipients I do know about have alibis for the time of her death. That is, Sheila Martin claims she has—and they're both fairly nice people who appear to have been victimized by Wanda.

"Gurley, on the other hand, is distinctly not a nice person, and he gets this special attention for trying to put the pressure on me instead of coming to me decently, like the others, and putting his cards on the table."

Lucy set the portable on the coffee table, closed the box of notepaper, curled her feet under her robe again, and said, "Suppose Chief Gentry insists on looking through the mail himself and finds both letters? How many years in jail can we get for doing this, Michael?"

"God knows. Be sure to wipe your fingerprints off both notes before you seal them. And take your portable down to a repair shop on your way to the office and leave it to have the type changed. Not the shop we generally use, and give a false name. Just a precaution," he added with a wide grin. "It'll be up to you to see that nothing goes wrong. Take a taxi, but get off a few blocks from where you're going."

Lucy took a sip of her thin drink. "I've learned how to be cautious in a little thing like that," she said. "I'm worried about Chief Gentry and the morning mail."

"Don't, angel. After all, it *is* my office and my mail, and Gentry has no right to see anything except one letter from Wanda Weatherby. I'll insist that you take the mail from the postman right in front of Will, and I'll tell you to sort it out and give me the one from Wanda. He'll be watching, so shuffle through them fast until you come to the one you addressed tonight. Don't, for God's sake, make a mistake and hand me *her* letter instead. It will be addressed in the same elite type and in an envelope just about this size, and may or may not have a return address. Watch out for that."

Lucy picked up the envelope, carefully noted the two letters she had exed out, and said, "I'll watch out, all right. I hate messy typing." She plucked a cocktail napkin from a decorative holder on the table and began rubbing it over the portions of the notes where she had handled it. She asked, "Is this all right for eliminating fingerprints?"

"Sure. But rub hard where you touched it, and on both sides. The envelope, too."

Lucy worked silently. She was disturbed, but she knew that any argument would be futile. She used the paper napkin when she folded them to place them in the envelope. She was tucking the notepaper inside when she turned to Shayne and said, "If I seal it now, how are we

going to get the thousand dollars Wanda Weatherby says
is inside?"

"I almost forgot that," he admitted. "You got a checkbook handy?"

"Yes—but what good will that do? I haven't got a
thousand—"

"Get it. And don't worry."

Lucy's eyes were deeply puzzled, but she went into her
bedroom and returned with a small checkbook on the
First National Bank of Miami.

"Write a check for a grand, payable to me," Shayne
directed. "Date it as of yesterday."

"That's about seven hundred dollars more than I have
in my checking-account," Lucy protested.

"You're going to sign Wanda Weatherby's name to it,
angel," he told her with a wide grin.

"How do you know she banks at the First National?"
she protested. "And don't forget that Chief Gentry saw
her bank stubs and will recognize the signature as a forgery
as soon as he sees it."

"Those are chances we have to take," he said blithely.

"Chances *I* have to take. I don't see *you* forging anything."

"It's not much of a chance," he comforted her. "I'll try
to hang on to the check. It is my property, and Gentry already expects a check to be enclosed, so there's no reason
for him to insist upon examining it."

"All right, but darn it, Michael, I don't like it. I'll never
understand why you get yourself into a spot where you
have to pull a stunt like this." She unfolded the checkbook, got a fountain pen from the desk drawer, and deliberately filled in the blanks with a broad backhand that
was exactly the opposite of her fine Spencerian hand-

writing.

Shayne said, "It's guys like Gentry who force me to take measures like this, and I don't like it. But a private detective has to protect his clients." He stood up and stretched his long body.

"You'll need a stamp on the envelope," Lucy reminded him, and again disappeared into her bedroom, taking the envelope with her. She moistened the stamp on a wet washrag, pasted it on, and carefully sealed it with a piece of tissue. She carried it into the living-room, holding the envelope in the tissue. She said, "Please be careful, Michael," holding the letter out to him.

He took it and put it in his pocket. "I'm always careful. Don't worry."

"But Jack Gurley is going to be awfully angry if he ever finds out you suppressed the letters accusing other people and you gave only his name to the police."

"I've had guys like Gurley sore at me before. You get some sleep so you'll be sure to reach the office ahead of the postman." He kissed her lightly on the forehead, patted her shoulder, and strode out.

CHAPTER ELEVEN

SHAYNE STOPPED at the main post office and dropped the letter in the slot for local mail, then drove toward his apartment. He felt weary, both physically and mentally, from traveling in too many concentric circles. And there was still Donald Henderson waiting to see him.

Henderson was a type of man he detested, though he had never met him personally. A self-professed humanitarian and loudmouthed proclaimer of the inalienable rights of the humblest citizen to life, liberty, and happiness, yet he was owner of the largest and scurviest slum section in the city, and therefore a bitter and articulate foe of any plan for public housing or slum clearance. His tenants, he was wont to proclaim stridently at civic meetings, had the same rights as any other citizen to hang onto their snug little nests in his crummy tenements and to resist every effort of a totalitarian government bureau to regiment them into more pleasant and comfortable living-quarters at rents no higher than they paid to him for the squalid surroundings in which they now existed.

It would have been more fun and probably a greater public service, Shayne told himself, to have put Henderson's name in the letter he intended to foist onto Gentry, instead of sending the police after Jack Gurley. He didn't know, of course, that Henderson had actually received one of Wanda's carbon copies, but from what the man had said over the telephone, he suspected that to be the case.

It was too late for that now. Perhaps there would be a

story in it that Timothy Rourke could use in his paper later.

He turned off the avenue and drove past the side hotel entrance to the driveway that led to a row of wooden garages maintained for the use of permanent guests. The double doors of his garage stood open. He slowed and made a wide turn, heading into the opening smoothly and without conscious thought.

There wasn't time for conscious thought as the long hood went through the doorway and headlight beams sprayed out to reveal momentarily the two men hugged against the front wall on either side of the opening.

There was a flash of reflected light from metal on the right, and close beside the car on his left Shayne glimpsed the figure and face of a masked man with a short-barreled shotgun held at approximately the position of port arms.

That was all. There was a split second between the realization that he had driven into a perfect ambush and the moment when his car would halt with its bumper against the rear wall. Shayne's foot was on the brake and his motor was idling. There was no time for calculation or thought. There was only that instant between life and the certainty of death.

It was probably well for Shayne that his mind was numbed with fatigue and practically in a subconscious state. His reaction to danger was wholly reflex and due to a lifetime of training in the specialized art of staying alive in the midst of danger.

His big foot slid from the brake to the throttle. The ultra-modern Hydromatic gear shifted as swiftly into low gear and the powerful motor roared thunderously.

There was a splintering crash of ripped wood and the screech of protesting nails from two-by-four joists and flimsy clapboards as the heavy car charged through the wall and into the alley beyond.

Protected by unbreakable glass and a steel body, Shayne was hunched over the wheel and fully conscious as he went through. His foot left the throttle to brake the car as he wrenched the wheel to the right with all his strength, grazing the rear of another garage on the opposite side of the alley. There was the blast of a shotgun behind him and the sharper barking of a heavy automatic.

Then his car was racing down the alley, and there was silence behind him. Not more than two seconds could have elapsed since he first sighted the lurking gunmen.

Shayne's mouth was set in grim lines as he slowed a trifle for the alley exit. He swung sharply in the wrong direction on a one-way street for a block, and again in the wrong direction at the next intersection which took him back to the hotel entrance.

He slid to the curb on screaming tires and leaped out, went through the open door with long strides to confront the white-faced clerk at the desk who exclaimed, "Good heavens, Mr. Shayne, did you hear that noise? Sounded like a building falling down—and then shooting."

"Right." Shayne's eyes were bleak and the lines were deep in his cheeks. "Get the police on the phone."

As the clerk whirled to the switchboard, a portly man arose from a deep chair near the elevator and came toward him, saying petulantly, "Shayne? I've been waiting here for hours—"

"You can wait a little longer," Shayne snapped. He strode to a phone booth at a gesture from the clerk, picked up the receiver, and barked, "Mike Shayne talking. Corner of Second and Third. Two hoods just tried to blast me. It's probably too late, but put out a call to pick up any of

Jack Gurley's boys that may be wandering around and give them a frisk. Gentry still around?"

Upon being told that the chief had gone home, Shayne hung up. He left the booth and said to the openmouthed clerk, "Don't bother me if cops come around asking questions. Just tell them I said the city owes you for a new back to one of your garages."

"Was that what it was, Mr. Shayne? Good Lord, I heard that terrible crash and then the shooting, and I didn't know what it was."

Shayne grinned slowly and took out a handkerchief to mop sweat from his face. "They were waiting for me inside the garage, and I had to keep on going. Maybe you'll have a chance to back my car around into the drive after a while."

"Sure. Gee, you are lucky, Mr. Shayne."

"Yeah. And right now I need a drink."

He turned away to be intercepted by Donald Henderson who told him importantly, "I hope I may have a word with you now, Shayne. I've wasted the entire evening trying to contact you."

Shayne said pleasantly, "That's too damned bad. Come on up and waste some more time if you're in the mood." He went to the elevator, and Henderson followed him.

Upstairs, Shayne went down the corridor without speaking and unlocked his door. He switched on the lights, tossed his hat at a hook on the wall, and sauntered toward the liquor cabinet, saying over his shoulder, "I need a drink. Have one?"

"No thank you," Henderson said stiffly. He walked to the center of the room and watched disapprovingly while the detective poured four ounces of cognac and lifted it to sniff the bouquet approvingly.

"Really, Shayne," Henderson complained, "I hope you don't intend to drink all that. I have an extremely important matter to discuss with you, and I suggest that you retain a clear head to discuss it."

Shayne grinned, drank half the cognac, and said happily, "Nothing like a small snifter to give a man a clear head." He sank down in a chair, indicated another near by, said, "Have a seat and tell me what's on your mind, Henderson."

"It's this—this letter." He took a square white envelope from his breast pocket, and his plump hand trembled when he held it out to Shayne. "It was delivered by special messenger this evening. I didn't know what to make of it at first. Most extraordinary, as you will note. A hoax of some sort, was my first thought. Perhaps an ill-considered practical joke. A man in my position does receive many crank letters."

Shayne noted that the address was in the same type as that on the letters received by Ralph Flannagan and Sheila Martin. He removed the folded sheet of paper and glanced at the contents with disinterest. The wording appeared to be an exact duplicate of the others. He yawned widely, and said, "So what?"

"I don't think you read it carefully," Henderson protested. "It practically accuses me of planning to murder a woman who is a complete stranger to me. A woman whose name I don't even recognize." He leaned forward with both palms on his knees. "You can readily understand how upsetting it was."

Shayne shrugged and smothered a yawn. "If you didn't plan to murder her, why should it upset you?"

"That's what I told myself," said Henderson quickly. "I had a meeting to attend and I put it aside, thinking I might check with you later to see if you could explain it. Then afterward, while driving home, I turned on my car radio for the eleven-thirty newscast. I was absolutely horrified. It was ghastly. I kept thinking it was some weird coincidence, but then I began to realize the really awful position I was in. Because the woman is dead—murdered, Shayne. Just as her letter prophesied. And I stand accused of killing her."

"Didn't you?"

Donald J. Henderson looked properly horrified at the suggestion. He snapped, "Definitely not. I've told you I don't even know a woman named Wanda Weatherby."

Shayne said wearily, "I know. A lot of people have told me a lot of different things tonight. This meeting you claim you attended. What was it?"

"Our Civic Betterment Association. We had an important agenda tonight, and I presided. I must say that I don't care for your attitude, Shayne," Henderson ended stiffly.

"The door is right behind you." Shayne took a big sip from his glass. Henderson compressed his lips and was silent.

Shayne asked, "What time was your meeting?"

"It was called to order promptly at nine-thirty."

"And the members present can swear you stayed at the meeting how long?" Shayne asked.

"Until we adjourned shortly after eleven o'clock. I didn't come here to be cross-questioned, Shayne."

"Why did you come?" the detective asked bluntly.

"To put this matter fairly before you and ask you to use discretion after you open your mail in the morning and read this absurd charge against me. It's a fiendish plot to ruin me, that's clear," he continued sharply. "As soon as I heard that the woman had actually been murdered to-night, I realized that was the only answer. A dastardly plan to smear my reputation."

"Do you mean to say you believe the Weatherby woman was murdered simply to throw suspicion on you, and thus harm your reputation?" asked Shayne incredulously.

"What other answer is there? I'm afraid you don't fully understand the vicious elements behind the interests I have opposed in taking an outspoken stand against the misuse of public funds to subsidize housing. I have pub-licly stated time and again that this is the downward path to Socialism—or worse. Communism, sir." His voice was rich and rolling now, as fanatical as any soapbox orator in Union Square. "I have been marked for purging. This is exactly the sort of Russian tactics those scoundrels would employ. They are sneaky and treacherous and un-Amer-ican. If you believe in Democracy and are a true citizen of our free republic, you will not hesitate to stand beside me in this fight."

Shayne crushed out his cigarette and asked mildly, "What do you expect me to do?"

"Isn't your duty clear? Presumably, you will receive the original of this letter in the morning mail, with a thousand dollars to bribe you to play an unwitting role in their plot to ruin me. By refusing to be taken in by these under-handed tactics, you will strike a resounding blow against the enemies of your country and mine."

"In fewer words," said Shayne, "you want me to disre-gard the evidence against you."

"Evidence?" snorted Henderson. "That letter signed by a dead woman isn't evidence. It's base calumny. Observe the devilish ingeniousness of their plan. Quite likely the letter itself is a forgery. Yet the woman whose name is signed to it is dead and cannot deny authorship. There it stands as mute evidence against me. Once this letter or a hint of its contents becomes public, I am automatically branded as a murder suspect, despite all my denials, despite all the evidence I can put forward to prove my innocence."

"So I'm to tear up the letter from Wanda Weatherby merely on your say-so, and forget about it?" asked Shayne. "What do you suggest I do with her thousand dollars?"

"Keep it," snapped Henderson. "If she did actually send it herself—which I seriously doubt—she will never know. And if the whole thing is a forgery, those who did send it will certainly not dare to come forward and claim it."

Shayne laughed shortly and finished his drink. "And some people," he marveled, "have an idea that private detectives are crooks. You'd better get the hell out of here, Henderson. I'm going to bed." He stood up, loosened his tie, and began unbuttoning his shirt.

His visitor's mouth sagged open. "I'm afraid I don't understand. Surely you can realize the importance—"

"Of keeping faith with my clients," Shayne cut in angrily. "If someone pays me a thousand dollars for investigating you as a murder suspect, by God, you're going to be investigated a thousand dollars' worth."

"Even if it's dirty Communist money?" demanded Henderson.

"Even if it's dirty Communist money," Shayne told him flatly. He turned on his heel, stripping off his shirt.

"Suppose," Henderson suggested doubtfully, "I were to counter with an offer of double that amount *not* to investigate me?"

"I'd throw you out of here," Shayne told him, striding toward the bedroom and unbuckling his belt. He slammed the door shut, stripped off the rest of his clothes, and got into pajamas.

When he returned to the living-room, it was empty, and the outer door was closed. Shayne sighed gratefully and poured a final, small drink, then draped one hip on a corner of his desk and picked up the receiver to call a number.

He listened to it ring several times before Henry Black's sleepy voice came over the wire.

"Mike Shayne, Hank," he said briskly. "You got anything on tomorrow morning?"

"You mean this morning? My God, Mike—"

"This morning," Shayne agreed.

"Nothing but a lousy hang-over," Black told him.

"Mathews still with you?"

"My checkbook says he is, but sometimes I wonder."

"You and Mathews have a job," Shayne broke in. "Get around to the post office early—before any mail deliveries start out—and get on the tail of the postman who makes the early delivery to my office building. Stay on his tail, Hank, until he reaches my office."

"Wait a minute. Which postman is he? How'll I know?"

"If a smart dick like you can't get that information," said Shayne, "it'll probably be all right, because a couple of would-be hijackers shouldn't be able to get it, either. In that case, you and Mathews better be hanging around the street outside close to nine o'clock, because that will be their best chance."

"Hijackers? Is this a gun job, Mike?"

"Wear everything you've got," Shayne advised him grimly. "They tried to use a riot gun on me tonight, so don't spare the ammunition if anything breaks."

"Hey! Why ring me in on a deal like that?" demanded

Black in alarm. "If you know who they are—"

"I don't. But they do know me, and I might spoil the try by being around. Besides," he added happily, "I'll be paying you for the job while I get a little sleep."

He hung up, grinning over Henry Black's loud protests, and went to bed knowing he had done everything possible to make certain the mail would reach his office intact.

CHAPTER TWELVE

FOR ONE OF THE FEW TIMES since opening a downtown office in Miami, Michael Shayne opened the door precisely at nine o'clock the next morning. He was clear-eyed and jaunty, and he grinned at the sight of Chief Will Gentry seated stolidly in one of the straight chairs in the small outer room, and at Timothy Rourke lounging against the low railing talking to Lucy Hamilton, who was seated at her desk.

He said, "Greetings. You're up and about early this morning, Will. Hi-ya, Tim. Good morning, Lucy. Have these guys been bothering you?"

She smiled faintly. "Tim isn't quite his usual self on account of being chaperoned by Chief Gentry. They've been asking about the mail delivery."

"Oh, yes. I expect an important letter, Lucy. From a woman named Wanda Weatherby."

"Oh—yes." Lucy puckered her brow, as though just remembering. "She's the woman who telephoned you twice yesterday, Michael. Said she was writing you a letter."

Shayne said briskly, "That's the one we're all interested in. I promised Will a look at it, so bring it right in to us as soon as the mail arrives." He turned toward the inner office, adding over his shoulder, "The chairs are softer in here, Will."

"I'll stay right here until the mail comes," rumbled Gentry. "If there is a letter, I don't want Lucy holding out on me."

"Lucy wouldn't do that," Shayne protested. "And I promised you last night, remember?"

"I know," said Gentry placidly. "I've also seen some of your stunts in the past to wriggle around verbal promises. I'll sit right here by the door. Come on back, Mike. I want to ask you some questions."

Shayne shrugged resignedly, strode back, and twirled a chair around, straddled it, and faced the police chief with his arms folded across the back. "Okay. We'll horse-trade some more. For every question I answer, you answer one. Shoot."

"What happened at your garage early this morning?"

"I reported it to your cops. A couple of torpedoes were waiting to blast me when I drove in. So I kept on driving through the back of it."

"Did you recognize either of them?"

"No. The one on my side was masked, and I didn't take time to get a good look at the other one."

"What gave you the idea Gurley sent them?"

"You. You admitted leaving Gurley believing I had sent you after him to ask about Wanda. He's the type who would resent that."

Gentry grunted, took a sodden cigar butt from his mouth, and put it in a tall ash stand near his chair. "That all you got to go on?"

"It's enough. Any more questions?"

"What do you know about Helen Taylor?"

"Damned little," said Shayne promptly. "Probably much less than you do. She's a radio actress." He tipped the items off on his fingers as he continued. "She died around midnight, probably from strychnine. Prior to her death, her roommate found her in convulsions and muttering incoherently about Michael Shayne and Wanda Weatherby.

Said roommate telephoned me, but Helen Taylor was dead before I could reach her. That's all I know about the girl."

Gentry's agate eyes were hard. "That was the call you got while we were at your place," he charged. "You lied about it to get out of there without me."

Shayne nodded his red head. "I was in a hurry. The girl said she was dying, and I didn't want to waste time trying to explain things to you that I didn't know how to explain myself. If I had gotten any information from her about Wanda, I would have passed it on to you."

"Maybe." Chief Gentry's tone was grim. "The fact is that you did lie to me. As a result, the police were delayed in reaching her by fifteen or twenty minutes."

"The doctor who attended her will tell you that Helen Taylor was dying at the moment I received the call. The fifteen or twenty minutes didn't make a damned bit of difference."

"Why did you beat it instead of staying around to make a statement when my men arrived there?"

Shayne grinned. "I had a date waiting for me," he reminded the chief. "I had been rudely interrupted if you will recall. And besides, I instructed Mary Devon to tell you the truth about everything. There was nothing I could add."

"Will you swear that's all you had on your mind when you slipped away? Just a date?"

"That's all I had on my mind," said Shayne solemnly. "I hope Lucy won't be jealous, damn it, but I give you my word that I spent the next half hour very pleasantly in her apartment where there were drinks and other compensations for your and Tim's interruption when I was just getting to first base with Sylvia."

"All right," said Gentry grumpily, "if you'll swear you

still have no idea what Helen Taylor meant by linking your name with Wanda Weatherby's when she was dying."

"I swear I haven't the slightest idea. Is that all for now?"

"I guess so." The police chief looked at his watch and scowled. "It's eight minutes after nine. What time does the mail generally come, Lucy?"

"It's due any moment, chief." Lucy glanced up at the reporter who still lounged against the railing in front of her desk. "Why don't you sit down, Tim? You make me nervous standing there."

Rourke dragged himself erect and stretched his thin arms and torso. Turning to Shayne, he said, "While you and Will are keeping the vigil, I'll just pop inside and investigate your filing-cabinet. Still in the second drawer?"

Shayne nodded absently. "Pour me a slug of cognac while you're about it." He waited until the gangling reporter went through the open doorway, then said to Gentry, "It's my turn for a few answers now. What have you learned about Wanda Weatherby?"

"Practically nothing." The chief sighed and extracted a thick black cigar from his breast pocket. He wrinkled his nose with distaste as he bit off the end. "No letters in her place. Nothing to show where she comes from or *who* she is. She appears to have lived well and kept to herself, and we haven't turned up a single person who admits knowing her any more intimately than to pass the time of day.

"There is one thing," he went on slowly. "We've had two complaints from her at headquarters in the past week. Routine investigations were made both times without accomplishing much."

"From her—or about her?" Shayne asked with interest.

"From her. The first was a week ago. A telephone call

at eleven-thirty that she had a burglar. A radio car was at her place within five minutes. She was frightened and hysterical. A window in her rear bedroom had been forced, but the culprit had evidently heard her phoning the police and been frightened away. She insisted it was some-one trying to kill her, and asked for police protection, but could give no reason for thinking it was anything more than an ordinary burglary attempt."

"So you refused her police protection," said Shayne sardonically.

Gentry grunted and lifted one massive shoulder. "They turned in a report, and a cruiser was kept hanging around the neighborhood for the next few nights, but nothing happened."

Timothy Rourke came out of Shayne's private office with two paper cups in his hands. He handed one to Shayne, then asked Gentry, "What was the other complaint?"

"Day before yesterday—" The chief paused and moodily regarded the glowing tip of his cigar and warned, "This is confidential, Tim. Not for publication. She seems to have brought in a box of chocolates for analysis. Claims they arrived in the mail with no return address, and she was suspicious of them. She fed one to a neighbor's dog, and it died a few minutes later.

"They reported the analysis to her yesterday morning," he added sourly. "It was strychnine. Holbein went out to talk to her, but she flatly refused to give him anything to work on. Insisted that she had no idea who might have sent them, that it was up to us to find out and protect her from further attempts."

"What did you do about it?" Shayne asked.

"What could we do about it? Holbein is a good man,

but when she refused to co-operate, he could do nothing."

Shayne's gray eyes glinted. A phrase that had been repeated in Wanda's letters leaped into his mind: *He has tried to murder me twice in the last week.* He said, "That was yesterday morning. So she began trying to telephone me in the afternoon after getting no satisfaction from your department."

"Now, by God!" roared Gentry. "Let me tell you something, Mike. If you'd been in your office where you belong when she called, we might know something about this. Blame yourself for what happened if you're going to blame anyone."

"I do," Shayne said curtly, and for a moment there was silence in the small anteroom. Gentry looked at his watch again, and said irritably, "The postman would be late this morning. It's nine-sixteen."

"Has it occurred to you," Shayne asked blandly, "that someone might make an attempt to prevent Wanda's letter from reaching me?"

"What sort of attempt?" Gentry demanded. "Who knows she wrote it or what she wrote?"

"It was just a thought. If her murderer knows she mailed me a letter with pertinent information, he might try something. The strychnine in Wanda's chocolates reminds me of Helen Taylor," he went on swiftly. "How did she get her dose last night?"

Gentry shook his graying head soberly. "There weren't any chocolates around, if that's what you mean."

"What did the stomach analysis show?"

"Between a quarter and half grain. Probably swallowed very shortly before a heavy dinner which retarded the poison's action considerably. Around nine o'clock is the doc's best guess."

"At least an hour before Wanda was shot," Shayne muttered. "That would seem to do away with the possibility of murder and suicide on Helen's part. Have you traced her movements during the evening?"

"We haven't had much luck. Apparently she was in her room getting ready to go out—according to the Devon girl's story. We know she had an audition at eight o'clock, and is supposed to have left there about eight-twenty in high spirits. After that, it's a blank until her roommate returned around midnight and found her too far gone to be saved."

"What sort of audition, Will?" Timothy Rourke asked.

"For a radio show. The producer called us this morning as soon as he read about her death, and volunteered the information. He says she seemed perfectly well and in good spirits when she left his place, and he had no idea where she went."

"What's the producer's name?" Rourke asked in a worried voice.

"It's a good Irish name. Uh—Flannagan, I think. Pal of yours, Tim?"

"If it's Ralph Flannagan," said Rourke, "it just happens that he is." He compressed his lips and his cavernous eyes sought Shayne's imploringly, but the redhead was busy sipping cognac from the paper cup and refused to meet his gaze.

"Seemed to tell a straight enough story," rumbled Gentry abstractedly, looking at his watch again. He stood up and his florid face was grim. "It's now nine twenty-five, Mike. I checked with a couple of other offices here in the building before coming here. They say the mail is never later than nine-fifteen. How do you account for that?"

"Why should I account for it?"

"Because, by God, I think you've planned some hocus-pocus to keep that letter from being delivered while I'm here," fumed Gentry. "You gave it away when you suggested a while ago that something might happen to the mail. If you've pulled a fast one on the United States mail, I'll make it my job to see that they put you *under* Fort Leavenworth."

At that moment the telephone rang, and Lucy Hamilton answered it. Gentry paused, breathing heavily, to listen.

She said, "One moment," and held the instrument out to Shayne. "It's for you, Michael. Henry Black."

"I'll take it inside," he told her, stalking toward the door of his private office. He added over his shoulder, "You listen on that phone, Will. I think you may be interested in what Hank has to say."

Hurrying to his desk, Shayne dropped one hip to the desk, picked up the receiver, and said, "That you, Hank?"

"Right. I thought you'd want to know how your hunch paid off, Mike. Just a block down Flagler. Two hoods waiting in a car to blast the postman. They had him spotted, all right, and if Matty and I hadn't been right there and heeled, it would have been curtains."

"What happened?" demanded Shayne, hearing a quick intake of breath from Will Gentry listening on the outer phone.

"The postman got one slug in his shoulder. They're sending a substitute along with the mail. Nicky Calloni was one of the boys. Matty got him square in the heart. I don't know his pal, but he'll live, and the cops are talking to him now."

Shayne said, "Fine, Hank. Send me a bill." Then he said harshly to Will Gentry, "Still going to put me in Leavenworth, Will, for interfering with the mail?"

CHAPTER THIRTEEN

SHAYNE CRADLED THE RECEIVER and turned to face the police chief who came stamping in and exploded, "What did Hank Black mean? Why did he phone you?"

"You heard him," Shayne snapped. "Nick Calloni and another man tried to hold the postman up on Flagler. If Black and Mathews hadn't been on the spot, they would have succeeded."

Gentry's beefy face was a study in conflicting emotions. He said slowly, "Calloni is Jack Gurley's right-hand man."

"So I've heard," Shayne told him dryly. "But he isn't any more, according to Black."

"Are you saying that Gurley arranged the holdup? Just to prevent Weatherby's letter from being delivered?"

Shayne shrugged. "Why don't *you* try thinking for once? In the meantime, you might apologize for suspecting me of fixing something to prevent your seeing the letter. Unless you think *I* hired Calloni and his pal to make the snatch—and then put Black on it to prevent it."

"Damn it, Mike, if you suspected Gurley might do something like that, why didn't you warn me? I would have put guards on the postman. That's what we've got cops for. You didn't have to call in private ops for a job like that. It isn't going to look good."

"Because your men would have scared Calloni off," the detective told him evenly. "He'd never have tried it if they had been around."

"And he'd still be alive," rumbled Gentry.

"Exactly."

"Damn it, you mean you sucked him into making the try hoping there'd be a shooting?"

Shayne lit a cigarette and explained dispassionately, "I couldn't swear to it, but I'm morally certain Calloni was one of the thugs who tried to blast me last night. I'm also morally certain that Gurley sent him to do the job. By sending Black and Mathews to guard the postman instead of a couple of cops—or going myself, I pulled Calloni out in the open where you can see him. And you can cut the moral indignation about his death. If I'd done it *your* way, you might have a couple of dead cops. You'd do better to pin a medal on me," he added dryly, "and you know it."

"Some day," Gentry said gruffly, "you're going to guess wrong."

"That's better than never guessing at all," said Shayne blithely.

Gentry walked stolidly around him and picked up the phone. He said, "Get me police headquarters, Lucy," and waited.

Timothy Rourke lounged in the open doorway, listening with feverish interest. While Gentry waited for his call, the reporter said to Shayne, "Have I got all this straight? You had Henry Black and one of his ops guarding the postman, and they killed Nicky Calloni and shot another hood when they tried a holdup on Flagler?"

"Not for publication," Shayne told him flatly. "Not my part of it. Let it come out that Black and Matty were on the scene accidentally and were just lucky enough to prevent the snatch." He stopped to listen as Gentry spoke into the telephone.

"Chief Gentry. Get me Lieutenant Barnes." He waited

a moment, chewing on his soggy cigar stub, then said, "Barnes? . . . Take some men and pick up The Lantern. Jack Gurley. That's right. Find him wherever he is and bring him in. Don't book him for anything. Hold him." He hung up and turned away from the desk.

The three men heard the front door of the office open and a voice drawl, "Mawnin', ma'am. Sorry the mail's late, but there was a little trouble."

Gentry went out hurriedly, with Shayne on his heels. A wiry young man with a bulging mailbag was in the act of handing a sheaf of letters across the railing to Lucy Hamilton.

"I'll take that mail," Gentry said sternly, his pudgy hand outstretched.

The substitute postman turned and looked at him in openmouthed surprise. His mouth gaped wider as Shayne shouldered the police chief aside and said angrily, "Not that way, Will. This is still my office, damn it. Is that mail for Michael Shayne?" he demanded of the postman.

"Y-Yessir."

"I'm the chief of police," fumed Gentry. "I'll be responsible."

"But I'm Michael Shayne," said the redhead to the confused postman. "If those letters are addressed to me, you'd better hand them over."

"Yessir." The man thrust the sheaf of letters into his hand and fled.

"Now, by God, Mike—" Gentry began, but Shayne cut him off coldly.

"Stop making an ass of yourself. You'll see Wanda Weatherby's letter if it's here. But you're not going to paw through the rest of my mail at the same time."

Shayne passed the packet of mail to Lucy. "Go through

them and see if you find a letter from Wanda Weatherby. Give it to me if you do."

Timothy Rourke stood behind the two men, an interested spectator. Lucy laid the letters on her desk and began glancing through them. She studied the fourth envelope briefly and said, "Here it is," and handed her employer the square white envelope he had mailed to himself early that morning.

Shayne studied it gravely, holding it out for Gentry to see. "Here it is. No hocus-pocus. No sleight-of-hand. No nothing. It just happens I don't like to have a cop pawing through my mail."

He slid his forefinger under the flap and tore it open, took out the two sheets of folded notepaper before Gentry's eyes, and extracted the check. He glanced at the check and waved it in the air, saying cheerfully, "This explains the stub you found in Wanda's checkbook." He handed it to Lucy. "Better put that in the safe," he advised, "before Will tries to grab it."

"Keep the check," Gentry said angrily. "I want to read her letter."

"You shall," Shayne soothed him, "just as soon as I finish it." He unfolded the first sheet and glanced through it rapidly, raising his ragged red brows and grinning widely as he reached the postscript. He passed it on to Gentry, but warned, "Better get your blood pressure under control before you read the postscript."

He unfolded the second sheet while Gentry read the first one. His expression was grim when he handed it to the chief, remarking, "Now we know how Gurley knew what was in the letter and why it was so important to keep it from reaching me. I think you've got a charge you can book him on, all right."

Timothy Rourke had withdrawn, standing aside with a look of worried puzzlement on his long, thin face. Shayne grinned briefly, for the moment forgetting that the reporter knew nothing of the replacement of Wanda's letter by this forgery, and that he believed the letter Gentry was reading was the original copy of the one she had written accusing Ralph Flannagan of planning her death.

Rourke glared and muttered *sotto voce,* "I thought, damn it, you were going to do *something*—not just hand it over to Will like that."

Shayne shrugged and went past the reporter into his office, calling over his shoulder, "Let Tim see the letter when you've read it, Will."

He went to the filing-cabinet and pulled out the second drawer, took out three paper cups, a bottle of rye, and one of cognac. He poured two cups of rye and set them on the desk, filled his own cup with cognac, and closed the cabinet as Will Gentry came in, rubbing his heavy jaw reflectively and exuding clouds of noxious smoke from a fresh cigar.

Shayne gestured to the cups and said soberly, "Let's have a drink together and forget all this, Will. We've been at each other's throats ever since last night, and I don't like it. You've got to admit that I didn't hold out on you."

Gentry hesitated, then picked up the whisky. "I give you credit for a smart play in having Black follow the postman. That pulled Gurley into the open, and now, by God, we've got him." He tossed the whisky off, sputtered, and crumpled the paper cup in his palm. "That bastard has been thumbing his nose at us for years. I never thought he'd be dumb enough to walk into a murder rap. What the hell do you suppose the Weatherby woman had on him that forced him to bump her?"

Before Shayne could answer, Rourke strode into the office beaming happily and holding the two letters in his hand. "I don't know what kind of frame-up this is, but it couldn't have happened to a nicer guy."

"Frame-up?" asked Gentry.

"What Tim means, I think," Shayne said casually, "is that this has all the earmarks of a phony. We know that Gurley received a copy of that letter earlier in the evening, so it would look as though he's the one man in Miami who wouldn't have harmed Wanda last night."

Gentry's agate eyes narrowed suspiciously. He sat down heavily in the cushioned chair across from the detective. "Wait a minute, now. Sure he knew about the letter. And that drove him to it. If she'd been alive this morning she meant to come to you with whatever she had on Gurley. He had to kill her before she saw you. Probably had a man planted outside her house last night and heard her telephone you to come over in a hurry. So, that was curtains for Wanda."

Shayne wrinkled his brows thoughtfully. "I don't know, Will."

"Why else would he have risked hijacking the United States mail?" Gentry argued.

"Even if he didn't kill her himself," Shayne objected, "he knew this letter put him on one hell of a spot when he found out someone else did the job last night. That gave him practically the same motive for grabbing the mail as if he were guilty." He swiveled back in his chair and tugged at his earlobe for a moment, then added, "I think that's what Tim meant when he mentioned a frame-up."

The reporter drew a chair up to the side of the desk, sank into it, and laid the letters on the table.

Chief Gentry's cigar was dead. He leaned forward to lay

it in an ash tray, then asked Shayne, "You mean to say you don't think Wanda Weatherby wrote the letter? That someone planned to kill her and used this method of throwing suspicion on Gurley?"

Shayne said slowly, "If that check is good, Wanda must have written the covering letter. But she took the precaution of sending a carbon copy to Gurley as insurance against his harming her. It should have worked that way, but we know it didn't."

"Sure. But when he killed her last night," Gentry argued, "he had his plans all made for seeing that the letter never reached you. If you hadn't figured that move and had Black on the job," he interposed grudgingly, "he might have succeeded. I still say it was his best bet under the circumstances. We'll know more about that when we find out exactly why Wanda Weatherby was afraid of him."

There was a brief silence, then Shayne said abruptly, "Tell me something. Do you know whether private stag parties at the Sportsman's Club are sometimes enlivened with pornographic movies?"

"I wouldn't know about that," Gentry told him.

"I would," Timothy Rourke said. "The answer is yes. I never attended one myself, but I know fellows who have."

"Yeh," Gentry said with deep disgust. "Fellows who'd swear you were a liar if we put them on a witness stand."

"While you're checking Wanda's background," Shayne broke in hastily, "see if you can find anything to indicate she's been mixed up in that sort of thing. You might check with Detroit—all the way back to the mid-thirties on that angle. And also look for her husband in Detroit, though somehow I don't think you'll find one."

"Where," Gentry demanded, "did you get the Detroit lead if you still insist you know nothing about the woman?"

"I made that statement at eleven o'clock last night," Shayne reminded him. "It was true at the time. I am a detective, Will, and the word means one who detects. I made it my business to learn some things about her."

"And you're not telling me how you went about it," the chief said sarcastically.

"No. But I'm giving you what leads I have. You're better equipped to follow them up."

"All right." Gentry came heavily to his feet. "My department will do the work of convicting Gurley, and you'll sit back and collect a fat fee for the job."

"That's the way it goes, Will," he agreed blandly. "And thanks."

Gentry strode stolidly from the room, leaving the door open. Rourke followed him, closed the door carefully, then returned to sprawl in the chair vacated by the police chief. He said, "Damned if you don't do some fancy skating on thin ice, Mike. Tell me how in the name of God you fixed it to substitute a letter naming Jack Gurley for the one Wanda wrote accusing Ralph Flannagan."

"Even a newspaper reporter should be able to figure that one out."

"Damned if I can, Mike. I was standing right there watching you open the envelope. Even if you had Hank Black primed to make some sort of switch during the fracas with Calloni, I don't see how he could have pulled it. And I don't believe a man like Black could be hired to tamper with the mail."

Shayne grinned and punched a button on the intercom. He said, "Is the coast clear, Lucy?"

"Chief Gentry went straight out."

"Throw the lock on the front door," he directed, "and bring any other important mail in here—if there is any."

"There is, Michael," she said excitedly. "I'll bring it right in."

Shayne snapped the switch and swiveled back in his chair. Rourke compressed his thin lips in wordless bafflement.

Lucy came in with a square white envelope in her hand, placed it in front of Shayne, and confessed, "I was so scared I thought I would die when Chief Gentry almost got the mail first. And then when you waved that check in front of his face—"

"You were perfect, angel," Shayne cut in. "Let's see what Wanda wrote to me."

He tore the bulky envelope open and shook the contents onto the desk. There were five sheets of folded notepaper instead of two, and a check for a thousand dollars folded in the center. He glanced swiftly at the four letters, all identical except for the different names, and pushed them aside. He read the covering letter aloud to Lucy and Rourke.

" 'Dear Mr. Shayne: I've called your office twice this afternoon, but now it's too late to reach you before tomorrow, so I'm writing this letter of explanation in case I am dead before you receive it.

" 'Someone is trying to murder me, has tried twice in the past week, and the police seem unable to do anything about it.

" 'There are four people whom I suspect equally, though I haven't the faintest idea which one of them it is. I haven't given their names to the police because then I would have to explain why I suspect them, and that's my secret and will remain my secret.

" 'The only precaution I can think of which may frighten the guilty one into giving up his attempts is to write four separate letters, each naming one of the persons I suspect, and send a carbon of each letter by messenger to that person. In that way, each one will think the entire burden of suspicion will fall on him if I am killed, and will be frightened off—I hope.

" 'I enclose my check for one thousand dollars as your retainer to investigate my death if it occurs tonight, and to convict one of the four.

" 'If my plan works and I am still alive tomorrow morning, I will telephone you for an appointment.

" 'Sincerely hoping to make your acquaintance, I am very truly yours, Wanda Weatherby.' "

CHAPTER FOURTEEN

"FOUR OF THEM!" Timothy Rourke exclaimed as Shayne finished reading. "Our Wanda must have been quite a gal." He scooped up the four enclosures and shuffled through them, muttering, "Here's Flannagan. And a woman—Sheila Martin. And Jack Gurley, by God! He's here, all right. And Donald J. Henderson! Why, the old whited sepulcher. What sort of game has *he* been playing behind teacher's back?" His feverish, slaty eyes studied the notes spread out before him, then lifted to study the detective's face thoughtfully. "You didn't even bother to look at the names of her suspects," he charged.

"I had already seen copies of three of those letters," he answered dryly, "and I had every reason to believe Gurley was the fourth."

"You'd seen three of them, eh? So the gal you were necking last night was Sheila Martin, and not the Sylvia you pawned off on Gentry."

"It was purely impromptu," Shayne told him, glancing at Lucy. "I had to explain her in some way so Gentry wouldn't start digging."

Rourke nodded thoughtfully. "I'm beginning to get it. If Ralph, or any of the three others, had realized Wanda had named the other suspects, none of the four would have been so worried."

"That's exactly what must have occurred to her when she wrote the four letters. She fixed it so that each one thought he was the only suspect—which would be a stronger deterrent than if each had known that he—or she—was only one out of four."

Rourke whistled significantly. "She had a right to be worried, with four people after her blood. I take it that you fixed that other letter, Mike. Mailed it to yourself so you could hand it to Gentry. Wasn't it kind of tough on Gurley to single him out for Gentry to work on?"

"I meant it to be tough on him," Shayne growled. "The others at least came to me for help. Besides, he's the only one of the four without an alibi. That is, I haven't checked Mrs. Martin's yet, but I have a hunch it will stand up."

Rourke muttered, as if to himself, "Three out of the four have alibis." He frowned and closed his eyes, considered for a moment, then said, "It looks almost like—collusion."

Shayne nodded. "Could be. The trouble is, none of the three admits knowing the others."

"Could they all have had the *same* reason?" Rourke asked.

"If Flannagan is telling the truth about that picture some guy snapped of them at the motel," Shayne observed, "Sheila Martin certainly couldn't have had the same reason. And I don't think Gurley is the type to be taken in by a thing like the Flannagan deal. If he did shack up with Wanda and she had a picture of him, he'd just tell her to go to hell."

Again there was silence. Lucy Hamilton, who had been standing and listening attentively, drew a chair back and sat down.

Rourke's head was bent, his chin resting on his chest, his eyes closed. He straightened and said, "I'm wondering about Henderson. I like him for a suspect—the mealy-mouthed hypocrite. He's just the type to fall for the

Flannagan setup—only in more luxurious surroundings."

Shayne shook his red head. "Henderson swears he never even heard of the woman."

"Do you believe him?"

"No. But I have no proof to the contrary. And he has an alibi. That's something you can check for me, Tim. Someone on your paper must have covered the Civic Association meeting last night where Henderson presided. Check to see if he was definitely there all the time between ten and ten-thirty."

"Will do," said Rourke cheerfully. "Wanda Weatherby must have been quite a *femme fatale* to have given four such widely dissimilar people reason for wanting her out of the way."

"She evidently played the field," Shayne agreed. "But what we need is someone who actually *knew* the woman before we can begin to guess *why* four people wanted her murdered."

"What will Gentry do if he finds out you hoaxed him on Wanda's letter?"

"Jerk my license," he said soberly. "The only way I can justify covering up for those three is to prove them innocent." He pushed his chair back and stood up. "Suppose you make a start, Tim, by checking Henderson's alibi. Don't just take the word of one reporter, but get hold of a couple of other people who were at the meeting. Then I'd like to meet you at the paper in about an hour and go through every damned thing in your morgue on Gurley." He paused, turned to Lucy Hamilton, and said, "You can reach me there if anything comes up."

"What will you be doing and where can I reach you in the meantime—in case Chief Gentry wants you, Michael?"

"Checking on Sheila Martin's alibi and satisfying myself that she really does love her husband enough that the threat of raking up a past mistake was sufficient motive for her to commit murder. But don't tell Gentry *that*," he added with a broad grin.

Rourke was walking out of the room with him. The reporter stopped suddenly, snapped his fingers, and turned to Shayne with a wide, crinkled grin. "In all the confusion, there's something I almost forgot, Mike. What's this about you going on the radio?"

Shayne stopped, and frowned. "What do you mean?"

"Or is it television? You know, one of those private-eye programs." Rourke struck an attitude and declaimed: "Tonight, folks, we bring you another exciting adventure in the life of Michael Shayne, redheaded, hard-fisted private eye of Miami, Florida. Scourge of the underworld and the darling of gangsters' molls, we bring you Michael Shayne in one of his most exciting adventures."

"What the hell are you talking about?" Shayne demanded irritably.

Rourke dropped his pose and said seriously, "It's a swell idea, Mike. You could play the lead yourself. The only honest-to-God real-life detective on radio, with Lucy playing the part of your ever-loving secretary. You'd have everything the other shows have got, plus the fact that it would be *real*."

Lucy came up behind them and said breathlessly, "I think it would be a wonderful idea, Michael. They could dramatize your cases from our files. Are you really thinking about it?"

Shayne looked from Lucy to Rourke, a puzzled frown between his eyes. "It's news to me. Where did you get the idea, Tim?"

"Hasn't anyone approached you about it?" the reporter

asked seriously.

Shayne snorted. "No. What makes you think they have?"

Rourke searched his friend's face, said, "You wouldn't kid me, Mike?"

"I wouldn't kid you," he retorted, and again demanded, "Where did you get the idea?"

"Why—a girl I know who's been doing some television work called me early this morning to ask me if there was any chance of her meeting you to see if she could get on the program. She knows I'm a friend of yours, and said she's heard the program was being set up, and wanted an inside track."

Shayne tugged at his left earlobe thoughtfully. "You say this girl is in television? I thought all the shows in Miami were on film."

"Then there isn't anything to it?" Rourke asked sadly. "This girl is a nice kid. She's been in radio—"

"There isn't anything to it," Shayne cut in sharply. "I don't know where she got the idea, but I'd like to know. What's her name?"

"Muriel Davidson. I'll give you her phone number, but I warn you she lives with her mamma and is what is known, euphemistically, as a good girl."

Shayne snapped, "I'd still like to have her phone number." He took a small book from his pocket and wrote it down as Rourke repeated it.

Lucy said, "Don't be an old stick-in-the-mud, Michael. Tim is absolutely right. You'd be a lot better on radio or television than a lot of those guys. You could be *realistic*."

Shayne whirled on her and demanded, "You aren't in on this, are you, Lucy?"

"Me? Gosh, no. It's the first I've heard of it, but I think

it's wonderful. Would they pay him for it, Tim?"

"We'll stick to detecting, Lucy," Shayne told her before the reporter could answer. "Here's something I want you to do while I'm out." He reached in his pocket and brought out the envelope containing the clipping he had picked up in Wanda Weatherby's home. The name and address of the bureau was printed in the left-hand corner. He showed it to Rourke and asked, "Do you know how an outfit like this operates?"

"Sure. This New York concern is one of the biggest in the country. They cover every newspaper and periodical in the country, and will clip items on anything—at so much per clip."

"On what basis?"

"I think you pay in advance for a certain number of clips. Fifty or a hundred, or something like that. When that quota is filled, you can either renew your order or not, as you wish."

Shayne nodded and handed the envelope to Lucy. "Call them long-distance," he directed, "and find out when Wanda Weatherby started getting clippings on Gurley. If they hesitate about giving out information, tell them their client is dead and that it's a homicide investigation."

He turned and strode out of the office with Timothy Rourke a step behind him.

CHAPTER FIFTEEN

SHEILA MARTIN LIVED in a duplex apartment in the Little River section north of Seventy-Ninth Street. A little girl of four or five was playing on the front lawn when Shayne stopped his car and got out. As he went up the walk he saw a young woman sitting in a metal chair under a coco-palm just off the walk of the other entrance.

The woman stopped knitting and watched his approach with placid curiosity. She wore a neat cotton dress and had a thin, intelligent face.

Shayne took off his hat and said, "I'm looking for Mrs. Martin."

"She's out at the moment," the woman said pleasantly. "Gone down to the corner for a can of coffee. She'll be back in a few minutes if you'd care to wait."

"Thanks, I will." He dropped to his knees on the grass and smiled at the bright-eyed child who approached him with shy interest. He said, "Good morning. Do you live here?"

She put the knuckle of her forefinger between her teeth and nodded with a smile.

"Doris is shy with strangers," the woman said. "Don't be afraid of the nice man, darling, and take your finger out of your mouth. I'm Doris's mother," she volunteered, "and we live in this side of the duplex." Her dark eyes appraised Shayne openly, as though trying to decide whether he was selling something or had come to collect an overdue bill.

Shayne said, "I'm with a credit agency, making a routine check. Do the Martins own or rent?"

"We both rent. They're good neighbors," she went on quickly. "Mr. Martin has a steady job and is a good man. He works nights and sleeps late in the mornings." She hesitated as though about to say something else, but looking past Shayne down the street, she said, "There comes Sheila now."

Shayne pinched the child's tanned cheek gently and said, "By, now," stood up and said to the woman, "I'll meet her outside so as not to disturb her husband." He nodded to her, put on his hat, and went down the walk to wait for Sheila.

She was bareheaded and wore a peasant blouse and full skirt and tan sandals on bare feet. She carried a grocery bag and her pace slowed when she saw him waiting. She stopped close to him and said anxiously, "What is it, Mr. Shayne? Has anything happened?"

"Nothing for you to worry about," he told her lightly. "Thus far, no one else has seen Wanda Weatherby's letter accusing you. And insofar as I know, the police are not aware of your existence."

"Thank God!" she breathed. "Do you know who did it?"

Shayne shook his head and suggested, "Let's sit in my car for a minute. Your neighbor said your husband is asleep, and there's no need to drag him into this. And don't worry about what your neighbor will think," he added as Sheila hesitated and glanced at the woman. "I told her I was a credit investigator on a routine job. She'll expect me to ask you a few questions."

Sheila looked relieved, and went with him, got in the front seat of his car, and said, "Jane is a grand neighbor, but she does have an awful streak of curiosity."

Shayne closed the car door on her side and went around to seat himself on the other side.

Sheila asked desperately, "Do you think you can prevent the police from finding out—and coming here to question Henry and me?"

"If your alibi is okay, I'll do my best. A lot depends on your friend, Betty Hornsby. I have to establish exactly where you were between ten and ten-thirty last night."

"Oh, Betty'll give you my alibi, all right. I called her this morning and told her you might be around. She lives just three blocks from here—on Eighty-Fourth." She gave him the number, and added, "She'll remember all the places we went last night."

"I hope it works out," said Shayne absently.

"It will," she told him, catching his hand and squeezing it tightly. "But tell me what happened after you left me last night. You were in a hurry to get to a dying woman to find out something about Wanda. Was it important?"

Shayne drew his hand away from hers and said, "I don't know. She was dead before I got there. Do you know a couple of radio actresses named Mary Devon and Helen Taylor?"

Sheila thought for a moment, and said, "No."

"Do you know a radio producer named Ralph Flannagan?"

"N-No. I don't think so."

"How well do you know Henderson?" he asked abruptly.

"Henderson?" She hesitated, sucking in her underlip, and her eyes were round and questioning.

"Donald J. Henderson. One of the local big shots."

"Oh." Her expression cleared. "I thought I recognized the name. I've seen it in the newspapers."

Shayne shrugged and said, "Okay, Sheila. I'll talk with Betty Hornsby. If your alibi stands up, I'll do my best to keep you out of the mess."

She grabbed his arm and squeezed it tightly. "I'll do *anything,* if you can."

Shayne looked at her speculatively and she met his gaze without flinching. A pulse throbbed in her smooth throat from some inner tension.

He nodded and said gruffly, "I'll keep that in mind." He reached a long arm past her, unlatched the door, settled himself behind the wheel, and started the motor. Sheila Martin got out, hugging her grocery bag in her arm.

Shayne drove the three blocks with a frown of concentration on his face. He stopped in front of a small, homey cottage where purple bougainvillea and flame vine intertwined on either side of the door and ran rampant over the roof. The lawn was freshly cut and the property line was gay with blooming hibiscus.

The outward appearance left Shayne totally unprepared for Betty Hornsby when she opened the door to his ring.

Instead of the neat housewife he had pictured, with a couple of tots clinging to her skirts, he looked down upon a frowsy, fattish blonde with loose lips lavishly rouged. Her hair was rolled in metal curlers, and she wore a wraparound kimono of flowered silk that accentuated her uncorseted figure.

She said, "Come right in," with a simpering smile. "Everything's in an awful mess, but I haven't had time to clean up after the party last night. You know how those things are."

Shayne sternly reminded himself of the job he had to do, and went into the hot dimness of a shade-drawn and cluttered living-room. The stench of overflowing ash trays and the dregs of last night's drinks filled the air. He took off his hat and dropped it in a chair, and politely declined Betty Hornsby's effusive offers of a drink.

He said, "Please sit down. I want to ask you a few questions."

"Of course," she said. "I know who you are now. You're Michael Shayne, the famous detective. Sheila said you were just terribly good-looking, with red hair and all." She sat down on a small sofa directly across from him and crossed her plump legs carelessly, letting the kimono fall away on both sides. "And she told me not to dare make a pass at you. As if I would," she added with a silly giggle, "looking like this." She touched the curlers with her finger tips. "But if you have a teeny bit of time, it'll just take me a jiffy to fix you a little drink."

Shayne tried to look genuinely sorry when he said, "I'm in a hurry right now. Maybe another time, now that I know the way. Right now I want to know about you and Sheila—what you did last night."

"It was terribly exciting," she told him. "Sheila was in a dither, but she wouldn't tell me anything about it except that she just had to raise a lot of cash before midnight. I had some people invited in for later, but Henry had their car, so I took mine and just left the front door open and the lights on and the liquor set out so they could help themselves. Then I drove Sheila around to everybody I knew well enough to ask for a loan. She finally told me this morning that she needed the money to pay *you* for a retainer, but she wouldn't tell me why."

She paused, caught her breath, and leaned toward Shayne, her pale-blue eyes greedy, her lids puffed. "It isn't her and Henry, is it?" she asked. "They're not busting up?"

Shayne said gravely, "It's a confidential matter, Mrs. Hornsby. What time did Sheila get here last night?"

She sank back and said, "She told me you'd want to know that. She came over at ten o'clock. I know for certain because I was waiting for the Helter-Skelter Boys to come on. Do you ever listen to them, Mr. Shayne? They're just a riot some nights. They come on at ten o'clock and the announcer was just introducing them when Sheila came in. So, I went right out to help her raise the money, because she's awfully sweet and I'd do anything for her."

"Where did you go first?" Shayne queried.

"To Mamie Eldon's. That's over near the Boulevard and Ninetieth. John, that's her husband, was asleep, but Mamie went through his pants and found forty-two dollars and gave it to Sheila. Then we stopped at the Crocus Bar on the Boulevard, and I borrowed ten from the bartender who is a real good sport.

"The Helter-Skelter Boys were just going off when we left the bar. They really should have more than a half-hour program. They are a scream, really, Mr. Shayne. There's this fat one—"

"I really must be going, Mrs. Hornsby," Shayne said firmly, and stood up.

"*Miss* Hornsby," she corrected him with a simpering smile. She got up and followed him to the door. "I was going to tell you all the other places we went, and—"

"I'll be back," Shayne promised, "if I need any more information."

"You do that anyway, and let me know next time and I'll have some cognac. Sheila told me what you like to drink."

"I'll do that." He stepped outside and breathed deeply of the fresh, sun-laden air.

He went down the walk without looking back, conscious that Betty Hornsby was standing in the doorway simpering after him, and wondering angrily how a woman like Sheila Martin could claim a floozie like Betty as her best friend.

He shrugged away his irritation, reminding himself that Sheila's friends were no concern of his, and drove back to the Little River business section where he stopped at the first sign indicating a pay telephone.

He went in and dialed the number of the television actress Rourke had given him.

A pleasantly husky voice came over the wire in answer to his inquiry.

"This is Muriel Davidson. Who's calling?"

"Michael Shayne, Miss Davidson. Tim Rourke gave me your number this morning. I'd like to see you."

"Michael Shayne!" She sounded breathless and a little disbelieving. "The detective?"

"Yes. Tim told me about your telephone call to him, and I'd like to discuss it with you."

"I see. Certainly." She turned off her excitement and her tone took on a businesslike quality when she said, "When would be convenient for you, Mr. Shayne?"

"Right now."

"I'm on my way to breakfast. Then I have to go on to the studio."

"Have breakfast with me," suggested Shayne.

"That would be wonderful. I'm near the Boulevard and Twelfth. You name the place."

Shayne thought for a moment, then said, "Meet me at Cramer's. Do you know the place?"

"Oh, yes."

"In fifteen minutes?"

"I'll be there."

Her voice had a hopeful lilt as she said good-by, and Shayne scowled when he hung up, realizing that she would keep the appointment, expecting to be offered a part in a radio show that existed only in someone's mind. He hated himself for not disillusioning her over the phone, but that would have required a lot of explanations that were better left until he could make them in person.

CHAPTER SIXTEEN

SHAYNE TOOK A VACANT BOOTH at the front of the bar after checking to make sure Muriel Davidson wasn't waiting. He ordered a double sidecar from the waiter, asking him to go easy on the Cointreau and heavy on the cognac, and telling him to set a place opposite him for an expected breakfast guest.

Muriel and the cocktail arrived at the same time. She was young and slender and astonishingly beautiful, with a well-boned face, lustrous dark eyes, and an outward air of demure composure which could not conceal the excitement seething within her.

Shayne half rose and smiled as she hesitated on the threshold. She saw him immediately and came to the booth, asking in a nicely modulated voice, "Are you Mr. Shayne?"

"I am. Miss Davidson?" She said she was Muriel Davidson, and when she was seated across from him, Shayne settled back with his sidecar.

She ordered orange juice, black coffee, and dry toast, explaining with a wry smile, "TV is lots harder on a girl's diet than radio."

"I've heard that TV is tougher on performers than radio in a lot of ways. How long have you been working in it?"

"Oh, I've just started recently. Is your new show going to be on TV or just radio, Mr. Shayne?"

Shayne hesitated a moment. He liked the girl's clear

eyes and the youthful honesty of her manner. He made up his mind swiftly and said, "That's what I want to talk about, Muriel. Frankly, the first time I heard of such a plan was when Tim Rourke mentioned your phone call this morning."

She blinked in astonishment. "You mean they haven't made arrangements with *you* yet?"

"I don't even know who *they* are," he explained.

"But that's impossible. They'd certainly have to have your consent, wouldn't they?"

"I should think so."

"I don't understand at all." Muriel hesitated, and it was evident that she was bewildered and terribly disappointed. "I was told it was all settled, and that they were casting the show and getting ready for rehearsals."

"Who told you that?"

She said, "I'm sorry, but I gave my word of honor not to tell, but the information should have been authentic. I understood that the girl who was chosen to play the lead would be unable to do it, and that there was a definite opening for someone. That's why I phoned Tim so early this morning. Things move fast in this business, and I thought if I could arrange to meet you and you liked me for the part—" Her voice faltered self-consciously, but she managed a smile. "It seemed such a good idea for a program. It *is* a perfectly wonderful idea," she went on strongly. "With your reputation and all the publicity you've had. It's a natural, Mr. Shayne. It couldn't possibly miss. Perhaps the producer who dreamed it up is holding back from contacting you until he gets an audition script ready and a show in rehearsal. That would explain why it's all so hush-hush. It's an idea that could be stolen by anyone. And it really is terrific. Any of the networks would grab it. A real detective in real-life cases," she ended, her dark eyes sparkling with excitement.

Shayne smiled at her enthusiasm. "Maybe. Suppose I promise you this, Muriel. If such a program does materialize in the future, I'll do my best to see that you are engaged for the job. In exchange for that promise, you tell me who told you about it."

The eagerness faded from her young face, and she shook her head despondently. "I can't do that, Mr. Shayne. I promised I wouldn't."

"Why?" he demanded. "Why did your informant exact such a promise?"

A frown creased her forehead and smoothed away. She said, "I don't know exactly. I imagine he was violating a confidence to give me the tip. You don't know how jealous and secretive everything is in radio and television."

"Was it Ralph Flannagan?"

"Oh, no." Her answer came forthrightly and without hesitation. "I know Ralph, of course, but just casually. Do you think he plans to produce it?"

Shayne shrugged. "He just happens to be the only person I know in Miami who is actively engaged in radio." He paused while the waiter set Muriel's frugal breakfast before her, then asked, "Does the name Wanda Weatherby mean anything at all to you?"

"That's—the woman who was shot last night."

Shayne nodded. "Have you ever met her—heard her name mentioned before in any connection?"

"No. I'm quite sure I haven't. It isn't a name one would easily forget. Why, Mr. Shayne?"

Shayne emptied his cocktail glass before replying. "I'm going to be absolutely frank with you, and this is confidential. I don't know how this hooks up, but it's definitely possible that the story you heard about me going on radio has something to do with Wanda Weatherby's death. Every move I make in my investigation brings me into some sort of contact with radio and television. That's why I'm going to ask you to break your promise and give me the name of the person who tipped you off about my program."

Again she frowned, and her eyes were puzzled. "I'm afraid I don't understand what you mean."

"I don't understand myself," he said irritably. "It's a possible lead. That's all. And I have damned few of them thus far. Did you know Helen Taylor?" he asked abruptly.

"Yes. Quite well. I was terribly sorry to read about her sudden death in the paper this morning. I saw her only a few days ago, and she seemed perfectly healthy."

"The morning paper didn't carry the full story," he told her gravely. "Helen Taylor was poisoned."

"You mean—murdered?"

Shayne nodded. "This is also confidential. I have reason to believe she was murdered by the same person who shot Wanda Weatherby. The person whom you may be protecting by keeping your promise."

"Oh—no!" Her reaction was instantaneous and positive. "*He* couldn't have— No, Mr. Shayne. It just isn't possible."

"I'm not saying your friend is a murderer," said Shayne. "On the other hand, would you protect him if he were? If he had killed Wanda Weatherby and your friend, Helen Taylor?"

"No. Certainly not. But nothing would ever make me believe that about him."

"If he can inspire such loyalty in a nice person like you," Shayne said persuasively, "he must be all right. But I need to know where he heard the rumor he passed on to you. That's all. It may be very important."

"But, Mr. Shayne, I'm positive he had no idea of anything like that when he phoned me," she said earnestly.

"Of course not. If he realized it might be important information in a murder investigation, don't you think he would want to tell me?"

"I suppose so." She sat quietly for a moment, then said, "Yes. I'm sure he would. It was Harold Prentiss who phoned me. He's assistant director on the show we're shooting now. He'll be at the studio if you'd like to go with me and talk to him right now."

"I'd like that very much." He looked at the check while she finished her coffee and the last crust of dry toast, laid two bills and some change on it, and got up with her, suggesting, "My car is outside."

"It's quite far out on West Flagler," she told him. "They have temporary offices there in an old building, and have fixed up a small studio for shooting interiors."

They went out together, and Shayne swung into the flow of traffic on Biscayne Boulevard southward.

The improvised television studio proved to be an old three-story wooden mansion near Coral Gables. Shayne parked in the spacious front yard beside a dozen other cars and went with Muriel Davidson up the rickety front steps and into a hallway which opened onto what had once been the ballroom. Now, it was a huge, bare space with electric cables overhead and underfoot, spotlights suspended from the ceiling and mounted on heavy metal stands. There were four large cameras on rollers, and standing at one side of the room there were two flats at right angles to each other, simulating the corner of a room, with a sofa and two overstuffed chairs intimately and cozily arranged. Two girls and a man lolled on the sofa and in the chairs which were surrounded by brilliant spotlights and cameras. A dozen or so men moved about them, gesticulating and arguing in what seemed to Shayne a babel of confusion.

Muriel said, "I'm afraid I'm late, and I'm not even made up, so please excuse me. I have to hurry. You'll find Harold in his office on the second floor—up those stairs and the first door to the right. And do explain to Harold why I sent you to him." She hurried away and disappeared through a doorway on the left.

Shayne climbed the winding old stairway and knocked on the door with a typed sign that read: *Prentiss. Private.*

A voice said, "Come," and Shayne entered what had obviously been a master bedroom, but now converted into the most untidy office he had ever seen. A state of confusion, it began to appear, was the natural habitat of television workers. Three desks were stacked with a litter of papers and scripts, there were two typewriter stands without typists, three filing cases with most of the drawers partially open, wadded sheets of discarded paper ankle-deep on the floor, and in the midst of it stood a bony and harassed-appearing young man talking excitedly over the phone.

He wore faded-blue dungarees, was barefooted, and his toenails were purple with polish. The blouse that hung outside his trousers was a violent pink with green elephants and giraffes chasing each other across his chest. He was prematurely bald, had a very high forehead, and obtrusively large ears. His eyes were deep-set and brown and melancholy, and his jaw was long and bony.

He fixed his eyes on Shayne with complete disinterest and continued to talk excitedly over the phone.

"I don't give a green gumdrop what you think about it, darling. I'm telling you that scene stunk up the place and we had to call in fumigators. And it's out." He waved a thin hand in the air while he listened for a moment, then said, "And nuts to you, sweetheart." He hung up, and in the same breath asked, "Who are you?"

"Mike Shayne. Are you Prentiss?"

"Certainly I'm Prentiss." Obviously, Shayne's name meant nothing to him. He turned and shuffled on bare feet through a litter of wadded paper and sat down at one of the desks with his back toward the detective. He rested his elbows on the desk and buried his face in his hands.

Shayne took a cigarette from the pack in his breast pocket, and the scratching of a match sounded loud in the quiet room. The assistant director continued to sit with his back turned, his face buried in his thin palms, and did not move or speak.

Shayne shuffled forward in the litter and eased one hip onto a corner of a desk a couple of feet from Prentiss, and said, "The name is Michael Shayne. I want—"

"*Shut up,* for the love of God!" Prentiss jerked his head up and stared at the redhead. "Can't you see I'm concentrating? What was that— Michael Shayne, did you say? That's a detective, isn't it? Like Nero Wolfe?"

"Only different," Shayne agreed. He took a long drag on his cigarette and asked, "Where did you hear I was starting a radio program?"

"That's it!" He snapped his bony fingers, then pressed a palm hard against his elongated forehead. "You're real, aren't you? Sure. Mike Shayne! Hard-fisted, cognac-drinking private eye here in Miami. Why shouldn't you have a radio program if you want it? God knows one more on the air won't make any difference."

"Where did you hear about it?" Shayne repeated patiently.

Harold Prentiss stared at him for a moment, then leaned back and lifted one bare foot to rest it on the edge of the desk. He wriggled his purple-tipped toes and said in disgust, "Isn't that a hell of a shade? I ordered magenta, damn it."

Shayne leaned forward and slapped him. The force of his open palm slewed Prentiss sideways and his foot slid from the desk. He recovered his balance, stood up, and said seriously, "Why did you do that?"

"Cut the posing," Shayne growled, "and answer my question."

"What did you ask me?" He seemed honestly puzzled.

"Where you got your information about a Michael Shayne radio program?"

"Oh—that." Prentiss waved both hands vaguely. "Someone must have told me." He cocked his head on one side and narrowed his sad brown eyes. "You'll play yourself, of course. It's a terrific idea. Stupendous. On TV you'll slay them."

Shayne grated, "Sit down and shut up."

Prentiss sat down and shut up.

"You can answer my question," Shayne told him, "or you can tell the police."

"I don't—think—I—understand," the assistant director said, frowning.

"I'm investigating a murder. Two murders. And it may be pertinent."

"Why come to me?" Prentiss dropped his exaggerated façade of preoccupation and became composed and businesslike.

"Because you telephoned an actress named Muriel Davidson this morning and advised her to apply for a part in such a show. I want to know where the rumor started."

"Who knows where any rumor starts? You can't keep a thing like that a secret. Not in this business."

"There has to be some foundation, and there isn't any to this."

"There isn't?" Prentiss frowned thoughtfully.

"None whatever. So, someone started it. Who?"

"God, I don't know where I did hear it. One of those things you pick up—"

"That's a lie," Shayne interrupted in a mild voice. "You wouldn't have been so insistent that Muriel promise not to reveal her source of information if it was just something you had picked out of the air. I want to know where you got it."

"I see." Prentiss sighed and compressed his thin lips. He drummed his finger tips on the desk, and asked with downcast eyes, "You say it may be important in a murder investigation?"

"Yes."

"I was afraid of that," he acknowledged. He sighed again, and said bitterly, "I was a fool to tell Muriel. But I've been trying to make her for three weeks without getting to first base, and I thought she might be properly grateful for the tip. The crazy things a man will do when his chromosomes get impatient."

Shayne said, "I'm waiting."

"It was a girl named Helen Taylor. When I heard on the radio this morning that she had died last night and the police wanted to know where she had been between eight-thirty and midnight, I knew I'd be a fool to involve myself. So I didn't. I kept my mouth shut."

"Keep it open now," Shayne advised him.

"Yeh." Harold Prentiss lifted his thin shoulders in a gesture of futility. "I took Helen to dinner. That's all. I took her home afterward and kissed her good night in a brotherly fashion in that horrible lobby of her hotel because she wasn't feeling well and didn't want me to come up. That's absodamnlutely all."

"Where did you have dinner?"

"At the Palm Villa. She met me there a little after eight-thirty, and I sent her upstairs to bed about ten o'clock."

"But she felt ill after dinner?"

Prentiss nodded emphatically. "She'd had a drink or two before I met her and was a little high. Then she got a tummyache. She thought it was the liquor on an empty stomach and then the heavy meal. Maybe it was."

"Do you know where she had her drinks?"

"No. I didn't ask. She was celebrating, you see, because she had just landed a new job."

"What sort of job?" Shayne demanded.

"In a radio show. She wouldn't tell me anything about it. Said it was a big secret, so I didn't press her. Then, while we were eating dinner she began asking me if I'd ever heard of Michael Shayne. I said I had, and what about you? Then she got confused and tried to cover up, pretending it was just idle curiosity, but when I kept after her she asked me what I thought about a radio program featuring you in person and your exploits.

"So, I said it sounded wonderful and that she'd be damned lucky if she could land the lead in a show like that. She denied that was what she had been talking about, but I thought I could read between the lines and was pretty sure it was, and she had been told not to talk about it. When I heard she was dead this morning, I thought what the hell, it was a chance for Muriel to get an inside track, and I called her."

"Let me get this straight," said Shayne. "First, Helen told you she was celebrating because she had landed a new job and refused to tell you what it was. Later, she began talking about me, and when you pressed her to give a reason for her interest, she finally admitted she had heard someone was going to do a program featuring me. Is that the sequence?"

"Yes. As nearly as I recall."

Shayne cleared a few facts in his own mind during the brief, ensuing silence. Helen Taylor had just come from Flannagan who admitted he had received Wanda's letter at seven. True, the radio director denied having discussed the letter with anyone, but there was always the possibility that he might have left it lying around where a curious visitor might pick it up.

"Then it's possible," he said slowly, "that Helen Taylor might have been interested in me and asked questions about me for some entirely different reason? Something she didn't want to tell you, when you pressed her for a reason, it's possible that she just made up the story about a radio show on the spur of the moment to explain her interest in me."

"It's possible, I guess," said Prentiss dubiously. "It's the sort of explanation that might spring into her mind, and one she knew I'd accept."

"She didn't actually tell you, then, that her new job was playing the lead in a mystery program?"

"N-No. I put two and two together and came up with that. Are you serious about saying there's nothing to this radio-program idea?"

"Absolutely."

"But that's fantastic, you know. It's a terrific idea," said Prentiss excitedly, waving his bony hands in the air. "It's a natural for television. My God! You'd be colossal playing yourself. Michael Shayne in person. You've got the looks and the voice for it. It's worth millions. Come here, man!" He leaped to his bare feet and trotted to another desk where he pushed papers aside to disclose a tape recording machine.

While Shayne watched in amusement, he turned dials and started wheels turning, then picked up a small microphone and thrust it toward the detective. "Say something —anything. I'll play it back and show you how good you are. I'll produce the shows on film. It'll be the biggest thing in television."

Shayne grinned and said, "Come back to earth. I'm a detective, not an actor. You'll have to go to the police and make a complete statement about meeting Helen Taylor last night."

"That's it!" Prentiss exulted. "That's exactly it. You've got marvelous timbre and resonance." He touched a control on the recorder and the tape whirled rapidly backward.

Before Shayne could protest further, Prentiss turned another knob and the tape rolled forward and the detective's voice came from the machine with startling clarity.

". . . back to earth. I'm a detective, not an actor. You'll have to go to the police and make a complete statement about meeting Helen Taylor last night."

"See how well you come over," the assistant director exclaimed. "We're in, I tell you."

Shayne stepped forward and looked down at the machine. "So that's how they work. I always thought you had to process the tape—or something. Had to have another machine to play it back on."

"No. That's all there is to it. I'll tell you what. I'll work up a short script right away and we'll make a real audition for you."

Shayne shook his head and said grimly, "Right now, you're going down to police headquarters with me and talk to Will Gentry. Do I take you barefooted, or have you got some shoes around?"

CHAPTER SEVENTEEN

HAROLD PRENTISS DID POSSESS a pair of sandals. At Shayne's insistence he reluctantly produced them from behind a door, protesting that he was needed at the studio and that it was outrageous to force a man in his position to go to police headquarters with no more relevant information than he had.

Shayne was adamant, and escorted him firmly down the stairs, waited impatiently while Prentiss shouted to someone in the studio that he would be back shortly, then took him out to his car.

Prentiss sat beside him in glum silence throughout the ride, and Shayne didn't attempt to question him further. There would be plenty of questions thrown at him as soon as he admitted having taken Helen Taylor to dinner the previous evening; plenty of unpleasant suspicion focused on him for having failed to report that fact to the police.

Shayne parked in front of the police station just across from the F.E.C. tracks. They got out together and the detective led the way in through a side door and down a hall to Will Gentry's private office at the end. The door stood ajar and he pushed it open without knocking.

Chief Gentry sat behind his desk chewing on the soggy butt of a cigar and frowning at a typed notation before him. He rolled his rumpled eyelids up when Shayne said, "I brought you a little present, Will. If I'd had time I would have wrapped him up in tissue paper and tied a red ribbon around his neck."

Gentry shifted his cigar, looked Prentiss over from his bald head to the purple toenails peeking through the sandals. "On him," he agreed, "tissue paper and a red ribbon would look good."

Prentiss cleared his throat and started to speak, but Shayne intervened. "He wants to tell you about taking Helen Taylor to dinner last night. Don't be too tough on him for not coming in sooner, because the morning paper just had a brief item about her death and didn't mention poison. I've got to beat it, Will," he went on swiftly, "and I've already heard his story. You turned up anything important yet?"

"Not much." Gentry motioned for the assistant director to sit down. "I just had this report from Detroit, but it's not much. Just enough to show you were on the right track." He looked down at the paper he had been studying. "Nineteen thirty-three is the only record the police have on Wanda Weatherby. Prohibition was on the way out and the rackets were busting up. In a city-wide round-up of one of the Capone mobs, a gal named Wanda Weatherby got caught in the net. No particular charge against her, and she was later released when the police doctor discovered she was going to have a baby. They have no further record of her."

"Was she married?" Shayne asked.

"No record of a marriage," rumbled the chief.

Shayne was silently thoughtful for a moment, tugging at his left earlobe. Then he reminded the chief, "Jack Gurley first came to Miami with Capone. Was he picked up with her in Detroit?"

"No. I checked that particularly. There's no mention of The Lantern."

"Have you picked up Gurley yet?"

"We've got him," Gentry growled, "but he isn't talking. He's sitting right on top of his constitutional rights and demanding that we charge him with something so he can have a mouthpiece."

Shayne shrugged and said, "How does he explain Wanda's letter accusing him of attempted murder?"

"He doesn't. He's not talking."

Shayne said, "Remember I mentioned a possible connection between Wanda and pornographic movies. I understand that business has been taken over by television methods, and Prentiss may be able to give you something on that. He's an assistant TV director." Shayne was on his way out when he dropped that casual bit of information, and he closed the door before Gentry could ask any questions.

In his car, Shayne backed around and headed for the *News* building.

Timothy Rourke was waiting in a corner of the City Room when Shayne walked in. The reporter had a thick cardboard folder spread out on his desk and was working through a nass of newspaper clippings and jotting notations and dates on a sheet of copy paper.

He looked up when the detective pulled a chair up beside him, and said, "I don't know what you're looking for on Gurley, Mike," irritably. "This file goes back to 1936 when he first showed up in Miami on Al Capone's payroll."

"I'm not sure what I want, either, Tim. But first, what about Henderson?"

"That bastard seems to be in the clear, damn it. Tom Merkle covered the meeting last night and took shorthand notes. They show that Henderson was definitely in there pitching from about nine-thirty until close to eleven. He presided, and had to recognize the speakers and all that."

Shayne said, "I thought it would be that way." He bent forward to look at the file on Gurley, and saw that Rourke had worked through the clips to 1942. "What have you found on The Lantern up to this point?"

"Nothing much." Rourke glanced at his notes. "He was first picked up in '36 on a concealed-weapon charge. In '38, he applied for a license to run a bar and was turned down on account of his past association with Capone. But in '40 he was getting respectable. He went in partnership with one George Stuart in buying a gin mill on the Trail, and since there was real money involved, there were no questions asked about past associations.

"He kept on getting respectable, and was married in '41 to a local girl by the name of Isabelle Lancaster. They had a big wedding and went on a honeymoon cruise to South America."

"Wait a minute," said Shayne sharply. "That was 1941? Just eleven years ago. Did Gurley marry a widow?"

"I don't think so." Rourke leafed back through the clippings and studied an item from the society page. "No." He read: " 'The bride is the only daughter of Mr. and Mrs. Samuel Lancaster of Coral Gables. A recent graduate of Bryn Mawr, she has been one of the prominent members of Miami's younger set,' blah blah blah. Doesn't sound like a widow."

"Does it say Gurley is a widower?" Shayne probed. "Or have you run across any mention of him having a child?"

"No." Rourke leafed forward through the clippings idly, then said abruptly, "That's right. He has got a grown daughter now, hasn't he?"

"She's engaged to be married, so she must be at least eighteen," Shayne told him.

"Here's something," said Rourke, lifting another item

from the society page and showing Shayne a picture of a youthful woman and a young girl of ten or twelve.

"Mrs. J. Pierson Gurley of Coconut Grove," he read aloud, "and stepdaughter, Janet, who has recently returned from boarding-school to make her home with her parents."

Shayne said quietly, "I think we've got what we want, Tim. You check the license bureau here and see if Gurley admitted to a previous marriage when he took out his license. And get Will Gentry on the phone."

Rourke glanced at him with feverish curiosity, but lifted his desk phone and asked for a number. In a moment he said, "Will? Mike wants to speak to you," and handed the receiver to him.

Will Gentry said sourly, "My God, Mike, where'd you pick up this pansy? He wants to put *me* on television."

Shayne grinned and said happily, "There's millions in it, Will. In the meantime, check back with Detroit on Vital Statistics for '33 and '34. Find out if Wanda Weatherby had her baby there, and who is listed as the father. What sex and name, and what happened to the child."

He hung up and said to Rourke, "This could tie up. I've been wondering from the first what the hell could be a strong enough motive to cause a man like Gurley to want to murder a woman like Wanda Weatherby. This could be it."

"Not so fast," the reporter complained. "You say Wanda had a baby in Detroit?"

Shayne nodded. "I hope she had it there. Will has a Detroit police report that she was released from custody in '33 because she was pregnant. That would add up perfectly for Miss Janet Gurley who is now on the verge of marrying into Nashville society."

"You think she and Jack Gurley were married in '33?"

"Whether they were married or not, if she could prove that Janet was her child and that Gurley was the father, think what a hold she would have on him. If they weren't married, she could prove the child illegitimate. And if they were married and not divorced, Gurley is a bigamist.

"Either way, there's plenty of pressure on a man like Gurley who is trying so hard to be respectable and who evidently loves his daughter. With a motive like that to back us up, it wouldn't be difficult to get a jury to convict Gurley."

Rourke demanded angrily, "For having a bullet put into the head of a bitch like Wanda who would desert her own child and then use her for blackmail?"

Shayne raised his brows and his mouth twisted cynically. "Everything points to her being a bitch, all right. But the law has never declared an open season on women like her." He stood up and went on gruffly, "You check the marriage license, Tim. If my hunch is right, this gives us three people with sufficient motive for murder. I still want a fourth."

"Donald Henderson?"

"Yeh. The guy who has never even met Wanda—who suspects the accusation against him is a Communist plot and that anyone who goes along with it is a fellow traveler," said Shayne sardonically. "Him, I'd like to throw the hooks into. I'll check with you this afternoon."

Shayne went out swiftly and drove to a parking-lot near his office, went up in the elevator, and found Lucy Hamilton putting on her hat preparatory to going out for lunch.

Lucy's eyes sparkled with interest when she saw the look of intense concentration on his face. She asked, "What did you find out, Michael?"

"We're moving, angel. Did you contact the clipping

service?"

"Yes." She removed her hat and fluffed out her hair, picked up a memorandum pad and read from it.

"Wanda Weatherby wrote them from Los Angeles a little over a year ago, ordering a hundred clippings concerning J. Pierson Gurley and/or his family in Miami. They began sending them to her in weekly batches, and about six months ago sent her the hundredth one. She renewed her order at that time, but shortly afterward gave them a change of address from Los Angeles to Miami. They've continued sending the clippings to her ever since."

Shayne let out a long breath. He said, "I've got one more job for you before lunch. Come in here." He strode into his private office, opened the Classified telephone directory, and picked up a pencil to run it down the agencies listed under *Detective Service*.

He stopped halfway down the list and made a check mark, went on slowly, stopped again, tugged at his earlobe, shook his head slightly, and went on to another name which he marked clearly and without hesitation. He stopped near the end of the list to make another check mark, then handed the book to Lucy.

He said, "Sit down at my desk and call each of these numbers I've marked. Ask for Ned Baker on the first one. Don't talk to anyone else. If you get Ned tell him you're—oh—Edith Lane. Anything that doesn't sound too phony. Ask him if he has a flashlight camera, and tell him you've got a job coming up tonight, and ask how much he'll charge to be on call between seven and ten o'clock to go some place and take a picture. Don't tell him what the picture will be. But hell, you know what I mean. I want to know whether he goes for the job or not."

"You're trying to locate the man who took that picture

of Wanda Weatherby and Mr. Flannagan," Lucy said with her usual efficiency.

"Right. It's the sort of thing you might go to a private dick for. Most of them in Miami wouldn't touch such an assignment, but the three I've marked might not be too scrupulous." He stepped away from the desk and opened the second drawer of the filing-cabinet and took out a paper cup and a bottle of cognac.

Lucy dialed a number and asked to speak to Ned Baker. After a moment she said, "I see. No. I won't leave my name. I'll try later in the week." She hung up and said to Shayne, "Mr. Baker is in Washington on business."

"I didn't like Ned much for the job anyway," he told her. "Try the next number I checked. Ask for Jed Purly." He took a sip of cognac and sauntered over to the window overlooking Flagler Street, gazed down at the busy midday scene, and listened to Lucy dialing the second number.

She said, "Mr. Purly? My name won't mean anything to you, but this is Edith Lane. Do you have a flashlight camera you could use tonight?" She listened briefly, then said, "I see. The thing is, Mr. Purly, I'm not positive I'll need you tonight, but I expect to. Yes. To take a picture?" Her voice thinned a little. "What do you care, if you're getting paid for it? I thought that was what private detectives were for. What will your fee be? That's right. I'll want you to be handy where I can telephone you between seven and ten and give you instructions. How much? That seems awfully high. Well—why don't I call you later this afternoon when I'm sure? Yes. Good-by."

She hung up and said to Shayne, "Mr. Purly is one private detective who hasn't too many scruples. He'll do the job for a hundred dollars and no embarrassing questions asked."

Shayne nodded soberly. "Jed would be my choice. But try the Worden Agency, too. Ask for Peter Enright."

Lucy dialed the number, got Mr. Enright, and began the same routine. But the tenor of her routine changed swiftly to the defensive as she apparently began avoiding direct answers to pointed questions. She said finally and stiffly, "Very well. If you don't want my business, I certainly won't force it on you."

She hung up and turned to Shayne with flushed cheeks. "He was downright insulting. Wanted to know who had recommended him for the job, who was I and what references I could give him and whether I wanted divorce evidence or what."

Shayne chuckled. "Good work, angel. That gives us only Jed Purly—if Wanda *did* use a detective instead of ringing in some friend. You run on to lunch. I'll drop in on Jed before he gets away from his office."

CHAPTER EIGHTEEN

THE PURLY DETECTIVE AGENCY was only three blocks down Flagler in a three-story walk-up. The office was on the second floor, between an insurance agent and a mailing-service. The door opened and a tall, angular female stepped out as Shayne approached. She was adjusting a narrow-brimmed straw hat on her gray hair, and Shayne stopped to ask, "Is Purly in?"

She said, "Yes," with a rising inflection. "I'm on my way to lunch. If it's something you think he'll need me for—"

"Oh, no," Shayne assured her heartily. "I just want to see Jed on a personal matter." He went on and opened the door, entered an empty anteroom, and crossed it to a half-open door on the other side marked *Private*.

Jed Purly was a short, fat man with a fringe of grizzled gray hair that ran around the base of his moist, pink scalp. He was leaning back in a swivel chair behind a bare desk with his feet propped on it, watching with interest a small black spider swinging on a filament from the ceiling light fixture.

He turned when Shayne entered, arched sparse eyebrows, and said, "Come in, Mike, my boy. Would that be a Black Widow, you suppose?"

Shayne grinned and said, "If she is and bites you, bite her right back, Jed. That'll teach her but good." He lowered one hip to the desk and asked casually, "How's business?"

"Not bad. I do pretty good on the crumbs big shots like

you can't be bothered with." Purly clasped his hands across his stomach and blinked benignly. "Sumpin I can do for you?"

"A favor." Shayne took out a cigarette and put flame to the end.

"Always glad to co-operate," Purly assured him affably. "What kinda favor, Mike?"

"Some dope on one of your clients." Shayne gave it to him straight, watching his face keenly beneath lowered lids. "Wanda Weatherby."

Jed Purly sighed and ran a palm slowly across his forehead, looked at the moisture on it, and said absently, "Hot as hell in here. Ain't that the dame that got bumped last night?"

Shayne nodded. "How many jobs did you do for her?"

"Never heard her name till I read it in the paper this morning," Purly told him promptly.

Shayne's nostrils flared. He took a long drag on his cigarette, blew out a cloud of smoke, said, "You're lying, Jed."

"That's no way to talk."

"It's the way I'm talking. I haven't time to horse around."

Purly shrugged almost imperceptibly. "Pretty busy, myself."

Shayne ground out his cigarette and stood up. He said, "Go right ahead with whatever you were doing. I won't bother you while I look through your files." He moved around the desk toward a wooden filing-case in one corner.

When he was two feet beyond the man in the swivel chair, Jed Purly spoke thinly. "That's far enough, bud."

Shayne stopped and looked over his shoulder as the chair creaked. Purly had a Bulldog .32 Ivor Johnson in his hand. His face remained outwardly placid, but a network of bluish veins showed in his cheeks. "I read the papers. All the time I'm reading the buildup they give you. You got Will Gentry and his cops in your hip pocket, and when you're not spitting in Chief Petey Painter's eye over on the Beach, you're catching the slugs from some torpedo's gat in your teeth and chewing 'em up for breakfast. Sure, I read plenty about how tough you are in the papers, Shayne. Miami's one-man crime-buster, by God! But you don't walk into Jed Purly's office and push him around." Jagged yellow teeth showed between thin lips in a snarl, and his eyes were venomous. "One slug in the belly will spill your guts just like any ordinary guy."

Shayne stood very still, watching Purly coolly over his shoulder. He said, "Wanda Weatherby was murdered last night, and I think you've got the evidence right here to convict her murderer. Don't be a fool. If you don't give it to me, you'll eventually give it to the police."

"Suppose I say I haven't?"

"Then I'll have to call you a liar again," Shayne said wearily. He turned slowly, keeping his hands in plain sight, expostulating. "This isn't the way to play it, Jed. That Weatherby stuff is dynamite right now. I know you've been sitting up here this morning figuring the angles—now that she's dead. But I'm telling you there aren't any angles."

"You're telling me?" sneered Purly. His voice shook with anger and with the frustrations of years, but the round muzzle of the gun remained implacably trained on the redhead's mid-section. "That's funny. Right now *I'm* doing the telling. Do you get that, shamus? For once in my life—"

Every muscle in Shayne's body went lax. He spilled to the floor like a rag doll and a bullet went over his head.

One arm shot out to grab a caster of the swivel chair. He jerked with all his might, tumbling the fat man out of it and on top of him. He got his left hand over the nickeled gun in a grip that held the hammer from falling onto the firing-pin, and lying flat on his back drove his fist into the plump face above him.

Purly grunted, and Shayne turned sidewise to dump his body on the floor, got to his knees to stare down at him, and when Purly blinked his eyes, Shayne hit him again.

This time, he lay still.

Shayne relinquished the revolver after carefully lowering the hammer and let it fall to the floor. He came to his feet and turned to the filing-cabinet without another glance at the prone figure.

He pulled out the bottom drawer and found several dozen cardboard folders, beginning at the front with one tabbed *Theron, S.* He thumbed through to *Weatherby, W.*, and pulled it out. The folder was thin, and he circled Purly's recumbent body to lay it on the desk. The contents consisted of two eight-by-ten glossy prints and the accompanying negatives.

The first was the picture of Ralph Flannagan and Wanda Weatherby, taken at the motel, much as the radio producer had described it. Shayne turned it face down after a brief glance.

His eyes narrowed and his features hardened when he looked at the other photograph. It showed Sheila Martin and Donald J. Henderson in a situation which would be described in a family newspaper as "compromising." It was unquestionably a late photograph of Sheila, and the background was definitely Wanda Weatherby's luxurious front bedroom.

The trenches in his cheeks deepened as he studied

Sheila's face and recalled her pathetic story of having been blackmailed because of a youthful and somewhat trivial indiscretion. He shrugged and closed the folder, tucked it under his arm, and went out.

He stopped at a bar for lunch and several drinks of cognac to wash the rancid taste from his mouth, and to consider every aspect of the case.

The two checks for $1000 from Wanda Weatherby and Ralph Flannagan were as yet uncashed. Last night he had given himself the pleasure of turning down five thousand from Jack Gurley, and it was now too late to retract that. He had also gallantly told Sheila Martin to keep her cash until he decided whether to accept a retainer from her. He had been sorry for her, and enjoyed the taste of her mouth. It didn't taste so good in retrospect.

He got up from the table, strode back to a telephone, called his office, and found Lucy in.

"There have been two calls for you, Michael," she told him rapidly. "I don't know whether they're good or not. Tim left word that no previous marriage is mentioned in Mr. Gurley's application for a marriage license. And Chief Gentry called. He wants to talk to you about Helen Taylor and someone named Harold Prentiss and said to tell you that Wanda Weatherby gave birth to a daughter in Detroit in December of nineteen thirty-three, named Janet. Father unknown."

Shayne said, "That's swell, Lucy. Now that we've got the case solved, it's time we started figuring where we're going to collect a fee. Call Mrs. Sheila Martin and tell her she has until four o'clock to get the rest of that thousand together. In cash," he added sharply. "I want it in my office by four. I'll be along."

He hung up and went back to finish his luncheon, and

the food tasted better than before he telephoned. When he left, he walked purposefully down the street with Purly's folder under his arm, glancing at shop windows until he came to the place he wanted.

The store he entered dealt in office equipment and had a display of the latest model Dictaphones and tape and wire recorders. An alert young clerk came forward with a smile. "What can I do for you, sir?"

"I'm interested in the latest portable recording-machines and would like demonstrations of various models."

The young man was eager to oblige. He began showing the detective the different models of both wire and tape recorders, explaining that they both worked on the same electronic principle which Shayne made no pretense of understanding, and that each model was carefully designed to perform best some certain function that the others did less well.

"The tape recorders," he confided, "provide the highest fidelity of recording. For that reason they are favored by musicians and for the recording of voices that are to be broadcast later. Radio studios and so forth. This small wire recorder, on the other hand, is used mostly for dictating purposes—where the dictation is to be transcribed later by a typist. It has an accurate timing device that shows you exactly how many minutes of the hour-long wire have been used at any time, and it is equipped with a forward and reverse foot pedal that leaves the typist's hands free at all times. Here, try it yourself. It's very simple to operate." He set a small microphone on a table and turned a knob to start the wheels revolving.

"You set these two knobs at 'Mike' and 'Record,'" he demonstrated. "Now say something."

Shayne looked at the small microphone a dozen feet

away, and frowned. "Don't I have to talk directly into it?"

"Oh, no." The clerk's smile was indulgent. "Not with electronic recording. Just speak in your ordinary voice."

Shayne said, "All right. I'm speaking. Will it pick that up?"

"Indeed it will." The clerk reversed the motion and the wire whirred swiftly, rewinding on its original spool. He shifted one of the knobs from *Record* to *Play* and started the wire forward again. Shayne's voice came from the machine with startling loudness and clarity.

When he completed the demonstration, the young man asked diffidently, "Aren't you— I think I've seen your picture in the papers. Aren't you Michael Shayne?"

Shayne nodded, and asked with interest, "How far away will the microphone pick up voices?"

"I was going to explain that, Mr. Shayne. In your profession, this machine would be wonderful because it has such a powerful microphone. If you turn the volume on full it will pick up the merest whisper as much as fifty feet away. From an adjoining room, even. And it has an attachment that allows you to make a direct record of both sides of a telephone conversation and for recording radio broadcasts by a wire directly from the machine. I should think this model would be perfect for a detective. It's small and inconspicuous, you see, with a carrying case similar to a portable typewriter case. It plugs into any electric connection and is ready to go instantly. Here's a booklet describing all the ways it can be used. Perhaps you'd like to look at it," the clerk added as another customer came in.

Shayne thanked him and began leafing through the booklet as the clerk hurried forward to greet the new prospect.

The text was lucid, replete with illustrations, and highlighted with sketches of people laughing at hearing their voices played back at a party; others with men soberly listening to the recording of a famous speech from a former broadcast. It was indispensable to the busy executive—and for the creative writer who awakens in the night and records an idea on the machine at his bedside. There was even a method of splicing sections of wire to obtain hilarious results by interpolating one's own heckling or comments into any recording at appropriate places, and at one's own leisure.

Shayne looked up and nodded when the clerk returned. He said, "I'd like to try this one out. Do you rent machines?"

"No. But we'd be delighted to have someone like you take it out for a free trial—and no obligation to buy," the young man assured him. "Use it for a week with our compliments, and then decide."

Shayne said, "Thanks," and asked if it could be delivered to his office that afternoon.

"Certainly, Mr. Shayne. In a couple of hours."

Shayne thanked him and went out with the instruction book in his pocket and Jed Purly's folder under his arm.

He stopped at the nearest bar for a drink and to lay careful plans for the remainder of the afternoon and evening.

He was sipping his second drink when he decided upon a tentative line of action. He got up abruptly, left his glass on the table, caught the bartender's eye and indicated that he would be back, went out and down the street to a newsstand that specialized in out-of-town newspapers.

There was one Nashville paper in stock, dated that morning, and the front page carried a brief wire service story on the death of Wanda Weatherby.

Shayne carried it back to the barroom, sat down, and glanced through the item which gave only the bare outlines of the mysterious circumstances surrounding her death.

This was the same paper from which Wanda's clipping about Mrs. Gurley and Janet had been taken. Shayne turned the pages, scanning each one carefully, until he reached the back page which carried theatrical notices and a listing of television and radio programs for the day.

When he left the bar he slipped the file containing the two photographs into the folded paper, tucked it firmly under his arm, and went to his car.

CHAPTER NINETEEN

When Shayne entered his office a little before four o'clock, Timothy Rourke was in the small outer room talking to Lucy.

"You just missed your friend Sylvia," the reporter told him with a saturnine grin. "She tried to think up reasons for sticking around to see you, but Lucy took her money and shooed her out."

"I did not," Lucy protested. "Actually, I feel sorry for Sheila Martin. She only had nine hundred and forty dollars. Do you really want to take her last penny, Michael? It seems awfully close to blackmail. Just because of something she did a long time ago when she was hungry."

Shayne said, "Don't feel too sorry for Sheila." He took the folded paper from under his arm, opened it, and took out the picture file. "If you weren't such a nice girl, Lucy, I'd show you a picture. As it is, you'd better take my word for it that the sob story Sheila pulled last night was carefully designed to gain my sympathy. She offered me that money," he went on angrily, "to avoid being the subject of a full-scale police investigation into her connection with Wanda Weatherby's murder. I'm giving her value received. Has a recording-machine been delivered yet?"

"It's on your desk," she told him. "Tim and I have been wondering what on earth you're going to do with it."

"You'd be surprised. It's a handy little gadget." Shayne grinned and waved the booklet of instructions. "Right now I'm thinking of making a recording for that program we talked about this morning."

"You mean the Michael Shayne story—for radio? Are you serious?" Lucy's brown eyes shone with delight.

"Not particularly, but it may have other uses. Don't you know some girl who has an apartment at the Courtland Arms?" he asked her.

"Why—yes. Marilyn Knowles."

"What floor?"

"The third, I think."

"See if you can get her on the phone. If she's in, invite yourself up sometime this evening. About eight o'clock would be best." He turned to Rourke and said, "Come on in and let's try out the recorder. According to this booklet, it'll do practically anything except mix drinks."

"Then junk the damned thing," Rourke advised as he followed the redhead with a gangling gait.

Shayne opened the folder from Purly's office and laid it on his desk beside the wire recorder. He said, "Take a look at those two pictures, Tim, and help me figure out some legitimate way to blast our friend Henderson—if I can't hook him for killing Wanda."

The reporter looked at the photograph with burning eyes. He whistled shrilly and said, "I see what you mean. This gives both Henderson and Sheila a motive for murdering Wanda. Why—if *his* wife and *her* husband ever got a gander at this—and—"

"Take a look at the other one," said Shayne.

"Our friend Ralph," Rourke observed. "Is that the ineffable Wanda with him?"

Shayne nodded. "Snapped by a private detective, all right, just as she told Flannagan that night at the motel. But I seriously doubt the story she told him about the detective being retained by a jealous husband. It was much more likely that she framed the whole thing."

"And the one of Henderson and Sheila, too?" he asked, studying the first picture again. "You think Wanda Weatherby stage-managed it?"

"It's a reasonable inference," Shayne said dryly. "It was snapped in the front bedroom of her house."

"Wanda must have been quite a gal," Rourke observed dryly. "These explain three of her letters. Have you figured out the Gurley angle?"

"I think so, though we may never prove it. I can't waste any sympathy on Gurley, but it would be tough on his daughter to suddenly learn that she is actually Wanda Weatherby's daughter, born out of wedlock. Especially now, when she's about to be happily married to a stuffed shirt in Tennessee."

The buzzer on the intercom sounded. Shayne pushed a button and said, "Yes?"

"I have Marilyn on the phone, Michael. She'll be home all evening. What shall I tell her?"

"That we'd like to pay her a visit about eight. Tell her you'll call back later if we have to change our plans." He cut the connection and turned to Rourke.

"Call Ralph Flannagan and tell him we're throwing a party at his place tonight to clean this case up. About eight o'clock, and there'll be—" He paused to count aloud on his fingers, "one, two, three, four, five, six, seven guests. Counting you, if you want to be in on it, Tim."

Rourke hesitated, puzzled, but he asked no questions. He lifted the phone, gave Lucy a number, and Shayne prowled around the room for a moment, then opened the recorder case while Rourke made the call.

He unwound the extension cord, plugged it into an outlet, opened the textbook to a diagram on the front

page, and studied it. He then plugged in the microphone
at the end of its long cord, and began testing the controls,
referring to the booklet for each move.

Rourke hung up after a brief conversation. "It's all set
for eight o'clock, Mike. Ralph is on pins and needles
wondering what's up, but I told him I didn't know any
more about it than he did. What are you planning to do
tonight? Who are the seven guests? And what has Lucy's
friend in the third-floor apartment got to do with it?"

Preoccupied with the instrument, Shayne turned another switch, but nothing happened. He looked up at
Rourke and asked, "Do you know anything about working these things?"

"Not a damned thing," the reporter confessed. He narrowed his slaty eyes at the detective and asked, "You don't
think you can make a recording from another apartment
on the floor above, do you? Won't you have to bore holes
and connect up a mike?"

"I don't know," said Shayne absently. "The salesman
said this particular model— Wait a minute!" he exclaimed
as the cylinders began to turn and the shining wire wound
smoothly from a small spool to the larger drum. "That's
the gadget that does it. It should be recording our voices
right now. See this little light," he went on, "that flashes
on and off when I speak? And here's the volume control,
Tim. You're supposed to keep that turned just high
enough while you're recording so the light flashes on and
off, but doesn't stay on steadily. Let's see if the salesman
was right."

He picked up the microphone and set it on the floor
near the door and directed Rourke, "Leave it there, and
you watch the volume control. I'll go out and close the
door and talk to Lucy. Damned if I believe any mike is

powerful enough to pick that up, but the guy swore this one would."

He went out and closed the door firmly. He said to Lucy, "Make a note of these names. I want you to call each one of them and insist that they meet me at Ralph Flannagan's apartment in the Courtland Arms at a quarter of eight tonight."

He paused while she got a memo pad and pencil. "Donald J. Henderson—Mrs. Sheila Martin—and a guy named Prentiss." He stopped abruptly and said, "No, I'll call Prentiss myself. He knows all about these recording-machines, and I'll need expert advice. You call those two, Lucy. If they give you any argument, tell them they can come willingly, or with a police escort. And I'll pick you up about seven-thirty. On the way to Marilyn's apartment I'll explain exactly what I want you to do."

He opened the door and went into the other room where Rourke was leaning over the machine, watching it anxiously.

"I didn't hear a sound through the door, Mike, but the light kept flashing on and off."

"Good." Shayne turned a knob from *Record*, to *Rewind*, and the machine reversed itself, spinning the wire backward onto the original spool with tremendous speed while the hand of the timer moved backward from three minutes toward zero.

He turned the knob to *Play* when the timer was almost at zero, and again the wire reversed and wound slowly onto the drum. They waited expectantly, but nothing happened. No sound came from the machine. Shayne frowned and twisted the volume control to *Full*. Still, the machine remained silent.

Shayne studied the textbook again, frowning in deep

concentration. "Look, Tim," he exclaimed, "turn that other knob from 'Record' to 'Wire.' It says that if you run it on 'Play' with the knob on 'Record' it will wipe off whatever is on the wire."

Rourke hesitated, and Shayne reached over and turned the correct knob to Wire position and the other to Play. Immediately there was a blast of sound. Both men jumped and stared at the machine in dismay. Swiftly, Shayne remembered to turn the volume down. Modulated, the voice became his own.

". . . so the light flashes on and off but doesn't stay on steadily. . . ." There was a momentary pause, then: "Leave it there, and you watch the volume control. I'll go out and close the door and talk to Lucy."

His recorded voice faded as he continued, "Damned if I believe any mike is powerful enough to pick that up, but the guy swore this one would." The final words were scarcely audible, and again the machine was silent. A moment later another faraway sound came, faint and indistinguishable.

Shayne scowled, reached for the volume control and turned it higher. Instantly the words he had spoken in the outer office, with the door closed, came through clearly:

". . . insist that they meet me at Ralph Flannagan's apartment in the Courtland Arms at a quarter of eight tonight."

They both listened tensely until the recording was finished. Shayne nodded triumphantly and turned it off, exclaiming, "Hell, this gadget is going to revolutionize the detecting business. Why hasn't someone told me about it before?"

"You're just away behind the times," Rourke told him. "These machines have been on the market for years. But what about this party at Ralph's tonight? Who's going to be there?"

"Henderson, Sheila Martin, Jack Gurley, Prentiss, Will Gentry, and you and me."

"How does Prentiss fit in?"

"He may get an idea for a Michael Shayne radio program," Shayne told him with a grin. "Also, he's the last man we've found thus far who saw Helen Taylor alive."

He answered the intercom buzzer, and Lucy Hamilton said, "I got Mrs. Martin and Mr. Henderson. They both agreed to come—Mr. Henderson under protest."

"Good. One more thing, Lucy, then you can go home. Wait— Hold it just a minute." He picked up the folded copy of the Nashville newspaper and consulted the radio page.

"Get me radio station WMAK in Nashville, Tennessee. I want to talk to the manager or program director, or someone else in authority." He closed the connection and said cheerfully, "You can beat it before I make that call, Tim. The less you know about what's in the book for tonight, the better you'll play up when it happens."

CHAPTER TWENTY

HAROLD PRENTISS WAS WAITING in the back seat of Shayne's car when he brought Lucy Hamilton down from her apartment a little after seven-thirty. He introduced his secretary to the television director and explained.

"Prentiss has been giving me lessons on operating the recorder. He'll go up to your friend's apartment with you to get things set while I drop in on Flannagan."

Lucy acknowledged the introduction as she got in the front seat. Shayne went around to the other side, settled himself under the steering-wheel, and no one spoke a word as they rode to their destination.

Shayne parked in front of the Courtland Arms and the three went in, with Harold Prentiss carrying the small recorder in its neat case. In the elevator, the detective punched the second-floor button, then the third. He got out at the first stop, grinned reassuringly at Lucy, and said, "It'll be okay, angel. Just settle down in Marilyn's apartment with a drink and let nature take its course. I'll come up with a full report when it's all over."

The door closed and the elevator went up, and Shayne went down the corridor to Flannagan's door with a lot more outward assurance than he felt, found it ajar, and pushed it open.

Donald Henderson and Sheila Martin were there, seated in chairs at opposite ends of the long room. Timothy Rourke and Ralph Flannagan were standing in the archway and talking together in low voices. They all turned to look at the detective, and Henderson came to his feet as Flannagan hurried to meet him, exclaiming, "Tim won't tell me anything about this, Mr. Shayne. What has been happening, and what—"

"We're still short two guests," Shayne cut in. He consulted his watch and added, "They should be here any minute." He brushed past Flannagan to nod at Sheila, then turned to Henderson and said pleasantly, "Very good of you to come. I think you've met Mrs. Martin."

"Certainly. Mr. Rourke—ah—introduced us a moment ago. No one seems to know the purpose of this gathering," he added with a noticeable lack of his usual oratorical intonation.

"Sit down and take it easy, Henderson," Shayne told him, and turning to Sheila he added casually, "Thanks for the money you left with my secretary this afternoon—but I understood you were short sixty dollars of the full amount. I'll expect the balance tomorrow."

Sheila Martin bit her underlip and lowered her head, refusing to meet his gaze.

Shayne wheeled away from her as Will Gentry escorted J. Pierson Gurley into the room. Gurley was immaculate in loose tweeds, his square face impassive as he stopped inside the door and surveyed each occupant of the room. He nodded curtly to Rourke, but gave no indication of recognizing any of the others.

Standing stolidly at The Lantern's side, Will Gentry said, "Hello, Henderson," studied Sheila's face briefly, then glanced inquiringly from Flannagan to Shayne.

Shayne put his hand on Gentry's shoulder and said, "I'm sure all of you are acquainted with our police chief, Will Gentry. Beside him is Jack Gurley who is under arrest on suspicion of having murdered Wanda Weatherby last night. And this is Ralph Flannagan, Will, who phoned you this morning about having seen Helen Taylor last night."

Gentry grunted an acknowledgment of the introduction to Flannagan, and Shayne resumed.

"I asked all of you to come here tonight because each of you has known Wanda Weatherby in the past and may be able to help us find out who fired the bullet through her window last night and murdered her. You and Gurley sit down," he urged Gentry, and as they crossed to seat themselves he glanced at his watch and went on swiftly.

"I picked Flannagan's place to meet because when I was here last night I noticed that he had a highly selective radio, and there's a program coming over the air from Nashville, Tennessee at eight o'clock that should clear up several things. You can get Nashville, can't you?" he asked Flannagan.

"Why—I presume so, Mr. Shayne," his host said. "I've never tried, but I pick up San Francisco and Denver without any trouble. If I knew the station and number on the dial—"

"I have a Nashville paper that lists it." Shayne took the radio program he had clipped from the paper and said, "The station is WMAK, thirteen hundred kilocycles. See if you can get it now. It's about three minutes of eight, and I don't want to miss any of it. There's a Bing Crosby program preceding it, so you'll know when you tune in the right station."

Flannagan said, "I'll do my best," his face a mask of confusion, and went to the radio.

Gurley came to his feet and moved aggressively toward the detective, demanding, "What's this about Nashville?" His voice was hoarse with worry and anger. "What's a radio program got to do with anything?"

"Maybe a lot of things," Shayne told him evenly. "Sit down and listen and you'll find out. Are your wife and daughter still visiting her fiancé in Nashville?" he added pleasantly.

Gurley doubled both fists and his square jaw jutted belligerently. "You keep my wife and daughter out of this. They've got nothing, by God, to do with—"

Chief Gentry was out of his chair and standing in front of Gurley. He gave The Lantern a shove, and growled, "Sit down and shut up."

There was a buzz of static from the radio and the unintelligible words and bits of music as Flannagan turned the dial to center it on the right station. Then he stopped when Crosby's crooning voice filled the room with "A White Christmas."

"That must be it," he said. "It's right on the setting you gave me."

"Thanks. We should get a station identification in about sixty seconds."

Harold Prentiss, who had entered the room quietly on sandaled feet, touched Shayne's arm. The redhead wheeled about and said, "You got here just in time. Meet our host, Ralph Flannagan. Harold Prentiss. You two have a lot in common, including the fact that you were the last people who are known to have seen Helen Taylor shortly before she died last night."

The two men nodded briefly and guardedly, and Flannagan turned back to the radio and tuned the volume higher as the crooner's song ended and an announcer came on with a commercial.

Shayne stepped back to the archway and leaned negligently against the frame where he had an unobstructed view of each person in the room. They were all sitting or standing, tense and listening, with various degrees of puzzlement and worry and curiosity depicted on their faces.

The commercial ended and a voice said, "This is your friendly voice for Mutual in Nashville, WMAK, with studios in the historic Maxwell House. Stay tuned to thirteen hundred on your dial for the tops in local and network shows."

Then there was a clash of cymbals and another voice declaimed dramatically, "What . . . really . . . happened? How often have you asked yourself that question after reading a news account of some dramatic occurrence in your daily paper? How often have you put the paper aside and said to yourself, 'That's all very well so far as it goes—but I wonder what *really* happened?'

"Tonight we bring you another story *behind* the news. What . . . *really* . . . happened brings you each week a person who *made* the morning headlines—to tell you in his or her own words what really *did* happen.

"On our nationwide première last week you will recall that we brought to our microphone a man who had been acquitted of murder less than twenty-four hours previously by a jury of his peers. Sitting comfortably in your homes, you heard him relate for the first time: What . . . *really* . . . happened. You heard the startling confession of guilt from the lips of a man whom the law had adjudged innocent—a man who is protected by our laws from being prosecuted again for his crime; yet he confessed his guilt openly and without remorse to a million listeners.

"Tonight, we bring you a no less startling revelation. The story of what . . . really . . . happened in Miami, Florida last night. Standing beside me in this studio is the one woman in the world who *knows* the true story—and who, in a moment, is going to tell you what . . . really . . . happened.

"Did you read it? Was it headlined in *your* newspaper? It happened in Miami, Florida. Wanda Weatherby was shot to death last night under mysterious and baffling circumstances. The police were without clues, you read, lacking any semblance of a motive for the cold-blooded crime, and with no suspects.

"You were told only that Wanda Weatherby died in her living-room with a rifle bullet in her head that had been fired by an unknown assassin lurking in the darkness of the night outside her open window. How many of you read the story and wondered: What . . . really . . . happened?

"Tonight you will hear exactly that—the true story behind this morning's headline—the most startling and dramatic revelation that has yet been made on the air.

"This is not a transcription. No portion of this program is recorded. The voice you are about to hear is that of a real person who is now waiting at the microphone to speak.

"Tonight: What . . . *really* . . . happened, brings you *not* the perpetrator of a murder confessing his crime, not a fugitive from justice, but a fugitive from *death*. Tonight we bring you Wanda Weatherby herself to tell you in her own words what really happened in Miami last night. After a few words on behalf of our sponsor, Camel cigarettes, you will hear Wanda Weatherby's own voice."

"No! My God, no!" Ralph Flannagan jerked the words out wildly, staring at the radio with bulging eyes, his features twisted in a mask of desperation and fear and insanity.

"It *was* Wanda," he raved in a strangled declaration. "I

aw her through the window. I know it was Wanda!" He whirled around, white-faced and trembling, froth forming on his lips. "Shut it off!" he screamed hysterically. "It's not Wanda! It couldn't be! There's—some—mistake—" He collapsed slowly to the floor, gibbering incoherently and sobbing, while a deep-toned voice extolled the virtues of Camel cigarettes over his radio.

CHAPTER TWENTY-ONE

SHAYNE STEPPED OVER FLANNAGAN and turned off the radio, turned to Gentry and said, "There you are, Will. With several witnesses to his confession."

"But you're crazy, Mike," Rourke protested angrily. "You know Ralph has an alibi. I don't care what you say, I have to give him one myself."

"Why did you shut that program off?" Gentry demanded. "My God, I want to hear it whether you do or not. If they've got Wanda Weatherby in that studio, who the hell was murdered?" The police chief was standing, his agate eyes cold, and jabbing a soggy cigar at the detective.

"Wanda Weatherby is dead," Shayne told him flatly. He nudged Flannagan's groveling body with his toe and said gruffly, "Get up and tell us why you killed Wanda and Helen Taylor."

"Hold it, Mike," Gentry rumbled angrily. "If the Weatherby woman is dead, why does a Nashville radio station announce she's coming on to tell a story?"

"Yeh," said Rourke, "and sponsored by a legitimate outfit like Camel. Turn it on and let's hear—"

Confusion grew in the room, with everyone muttering opinions and making demands upon the rangy redhead for explanations.

Shayne leaned close to Gentry and muttered, "Order some quiet, Will, so I can give you the lowdown and prove I'm right." He turned to Rourke and said, "Give me a hand getting your pal off the floor and into a chair."

Gentry roared, "Quiet—and sit down," while the detective and the reporter dragged Ralph Flannagan from his prone position and dumped him on the couch. Gentry resumed his seat and chewed on the soggy butt of his cigar.

Shayne stood before them and said, "The Camel advertisement actually did the trick. You see, a radio sponsor is so sacrosanct to Ralph Flannagan that he couldn't conceive of any trickery behind their commercial. That, coupled with the fact that it was his own radio, tuned in by himself and with no wires connected from the outside— it *had* to be an actual broadcast.

"That's why I tried it here in his apartment—so he would *know* it was a regular broadcast." He paused and turned to Harold Prentiss, grinned approvingly, and added, "You put on a damned good show. I began wondering whether it was real myself."

"I—I—" the assistant director began, but his Adam's apple seemed to catch in his throat, and before he could find his voice Ralph Flannagan dragged himself up from his slumped position on the couch and muttered:

"Don't know what got into me. Just went to pieces. I didn't mean—"

"You meant it, all right," Shayne broke in harshly. "Sure, you went to pieces when they said Wanda was there ready to start talking. Because you knew damned well she wasn't. But you thought maybe someone else was there that had seen you and knew the whole story. Like you confessed, you saw her through that window last night when you shot her."

"I didn't say that!" Flannagan raged. "I tell you I was all mixed up."

"You said it and meant it." Shayne turned to Rourke and went on in a tone of deep disgust, "Hell, Tim, you and I were both suckers to fall for his alibi. He planned it that way—to use both of us to alibi him."

"I don't get it. I was right here."

"Look—here's how he worked it. I got a frantic telephone call at ten o'clock from a woman saying she was Wanda Weatherby and begging me to come over in a hurry. She hung up fast—before I could ask her any questions. Ralph Flannagan made that call while you were right here in this room reading the carbon of the letter Wanda mailed to me. Remember what you told me last night?"

"About what?"

"That Flannagan was just getting dressed after a bath when you got here, and went back to finish after giving you the letter to read.

"That's when he made the call. From his bedroom. He had just shot Wanda Weatherby and hurried back here to meet you on schedule—and to telephone me to establish his perfect alibi."

"*He* phoned you, Mike? Impersonating a woman—and you didn't catch on?"

"He placed the call, all right," Shayne explained soberly, "but a woman spoke Wanda's lines. After receiving her letter saying she hadn't been able to reach me by telephone, Flannagan knew that I had never heard her voice. He knew, too, that I had never heard Helen Taylor's voice, and he hoped to fix things so I never would. He sent her away from here with a slug of strychnine in her stomach that he expected would kill her before she learned about Wanda's death and began to add up the score."

"You say it was the Taylor girl who phoned you at ten o'clock?" Gentry interjected. "Prentiss, here, claims he was telling her good night at her hotel at ten."

"That's correct. You see, the voice I heard over the telephone was a recording Helen made right here in this apartment, before she imbibed a couple of cocktails loaded with poison. I should have caught on as soon as I saw the recorder in Flannagan's office—standing close to the telephone—and when he told me he used it to record auditions. But I didn't know so much about the gadgets as I do now. I didn't realize you could record a scene like that on wire or tape, stand there with your hand on the switch ready for it to start talking into the telephone the instant someone on the other end answers the phone, and let it keep talking straight through, then break off and hang up."

"Wait a minute, Mike," Rourke protested. "You told me about the call and you said you interrupted once and she answered you. *That* couldn't have been anticipated in advance and recorded. Even Flannagan couldn't have figured out what you would ask and make her answer fit perfectly."

"Flannagan is a radio producer," Shayne reminded him. "That was a smart quirk, and it had me stymied for a long time. I know now that he had her pause to catch her breath, and that's when I asked, 'What are you afraid of?' And she came in fast, saying, 'Please don't interrupt me.' Hell, that would have been the perfect answer to anything I might have said. Yet, it gave the definite implication that I was carrying on an actual conversation instead of listening to a recording.

"There were a dozen clues pointing to the truth," he went on impatiently, "if we had only recognized them. Helen Taylor came here at eight for an audition, after Flannagan gave her a song and dance about a new radio program starring Michael Shayne, and swore her to secrecy. He prepared a script in which she called herself Wanda Weatherby and talked excitedly to Shayne over the telephone. They rehearsed it, made a recording, and he told her she was just right for the lead in the new series. Then they celebrated her success with cocktails, and she went away happy in the belief that she had landed a longtime job.

"Afterward, she had dinner with Prentiss while she was still happy about her good luck, and partially spilled the truth, so she believed, to him. Then she began to feel sick. He took her home, and she must have turned on her radio and heard the news flash of Wanda's death at eleven-thirty. She realized at once that she had been duped, and kept trying to tell her roommate, but was too far gone to do more than mutter my name and Wanda Weatherby's. Even with all that," he ended wearily, "I didn't begin to get the picture until this morning when Prentiss demonstrated how a tape recorder works."

All eyes had been upon the detective as he spoke. When he stopped, they turned to observe Ralph Flannagan. He was slumped on the couch, his face buried in his palms, and his stocky body limp and shaking.

Rourke asked, "How the devil did you induce a radio station in Nashville to co-operate—to broadcast a complete hoax like that tonight? I know you called them long-distance this afternoon, but—"

"I called to ask them for the exact wording they used in making a station identification," Shayne explained. "I didn't know but that someone in the room would be familiar with that station and spot the whole setup as a hoax."

"You're still talking in riddles," Rourke protested.

"I told you this afternoon that a wire recorder would do almost anything except mix drinks. One of the things it does is to turn itself into a miniature broadcasting station and actually broadcast over the airwaves anything that happens to be recorded on it. It can be picked up on any radio within a radius of a couple of hundred feet if it is tuned in to the wave-length over which that particular recorder is set to broadcast.

"Lucy has a friend in this building, so we plugged the recorder into an outlet in her apartment. Prentiss simply watched the time and started the wire running at a few minutes before eight, and then came down to see what kind of reception we were getting. We recorded everything you heard, including the last lines of a Bing Crosby song, out at Prentiss's studio this afternoon."

Shayne reached in his pocket and took out two sheets of folded notepaper and handed them to Chief Gentry. "Those came in another envelope from Wanda Weatherby in a later mail. Maybe she neglected to enclose them in the envelope you saw, or maybe they were an after-thought when she realized that both Flannagan and Henderson also had a motive for killing her, as well as Gurley."

"I'm holding Gurley," Gentry rumbled. "That hood of his should be able to talk tomorrow."

"That's up to you and the federal boys, Will. Attacking a federal employee is out of my jurisdiction. But getting back to my case," he hurried on, "Tim can tell you what Flannagan's motive was. You'll have to figure out Henderson's reason for yourself. *He* thinks it's a plot of the Communists to discredit him in his fight against public housing, but I have a crazy hunch that *this* picture might have something to do with it." He took a folded 8x10 print from his pocket and handed it over to the chief.

He had completely blacked out Sheila Martin's face from Jed Purly's flash photograph so that it was impossible to recognize her. Watching the chief's face as he studied the picture, he said, "If the Commies figured that one out, we'll have to give them credit for being smart operators. You can see they used Wanda Weatherby's bedroom for their stage-setting."

Carefully avoiding Sheila Martin's eyes, he said lightly, "And now Lucy has probably chewed her fingernails to the quick upstairs wondering how things went off, so I'll trot along."

He went out the door fast, while Gentry was still looking sourly at the picture and the notes, and before he could ask embarrassing questions.